AF488990

Toss My Greek Salad

A Nicholas Fenske Book

Based on a Screenplay by
Nick Fenske and Pete Hatzakos

© Copyright 2022 by Nicholas Fenske All rights reserved. It is not legal to reproduce, duplicate, or transmit any part of this document in either electronic means or printed format. Recording of this publication is strictly prohibited.

Table of Contents

Introduction

It was the early 2000's and Zeus Papadakis was like a lot of other High School Seniors; he was on a quest to get laid. An as he maneuvers to make this happen, he is swamped with real life tribulations. His father, Socrates, a real stickler for his son going to college, to get the education he was never able to do. His Graduation Night is marred by a series of misfortunate events. Undaunted by these setbacks, Zeus spends the summer working at his Uncle's Diner in the Outer Banks.

Zeus's newfound independence has him more confident in himself, yet the black cloud of misfortune hover over Zeus's head. This new confidence has come by the way of Head Cook at the Olympia Diner, Angelo. Angelo is no sense guy, whose been around the block, he befriends due to Zeus's Uncle's lack of presence at the Diner and Zeus's life.

As the Summer winds down, Zeus must now make a decision he had been putting off ever since the beginning of his Senior Year, does he go to College or work for his Dad and learn the family business.

Chapter One – Oral Presentation

High School parking lot, afternoon. Zeus Papadakis is pretty much the typical adolescent trying to get laid and figure out what he's going to do with his life after high school. He is trying to start his car, but it doesn't start. Miss Smith, one of his teachers approaches, then enters his car.

"Hello Zeus."

Zeus is caught off guard.

"Hi Miss Smith."

*"Only a couple more days
and you'll be graduating."*

"Yep, onward and upward."

*"That's something I
always liked about you."*

"What's that?"

"Your positive attitude."

"Positive breeds positive."

"Well, that and your smile."

"You know what I like about you?"

"Hum, let me, see?"

She looks down at her chest.

"My two big"

Zeus looks at her chest.

"Blue eyes."

*"Yeah, that's it, your blue eyes and
your sense of humor. I wish you were
a shop teacher and could help me
start my car."*

*"I don't need to be a shop teacher
to get your motor running."*

Zeus is intrigued with her statement.

"Really?"

*"Yeah, really. You'd be amazed
at the things I can do in a car."*

She grabs Zeus's stick shift and starts stroking it. We
see Zeus's eyes open wide. She stops.

"So, why weren't you in class today?"

"Um, you caught me, I skipped today."

*"That's too bad, you missed
my oral presentation."*

"Man, I'm sorry I missed that."

Sarcastically said.

*"Me too! Maybe I should give you
your own personal oral presentation?"*

Zeus is excited.

"Yeah, I think I'd like that.

Miss Smith looks around, gets closer to Zeus.
Heinz Duncan, 18, Zeus's best friend. He is the kid in
High School that knows a little more about life than he
should for a young man of his age. He backs up next to
Zeus's car.

"Aye! Yasuo Greek boy! How you are doing!"

Zeus does not respond, instead he grabs the steering
wheel.

*"That's Greek, it means... Nevermind
what it means, hey, jerk off!"*

Zeus continues to ignore Heinz. Heinz gets a concerned look
on his face and gets out of the car and walks over to Zeus's car.
We see Zeus's hands tightly grasping the steering wheel, we see
his face getting more serious, he's in a state of ecstasy. His
breathing increases and his head is going into a motion. He is
coming to climax. The windshield wiper fluid shooting its spray
on the windshield. Suddenly Zeus hears a tap on the driver's
window of his car.

"Bro, what the hell are you doing?"

Zeus is startled, he looks to the passenger, it's all been
a fantasy. He's embarrassed.

"Ah, nothing, what's up?"

"Whatever, freak! So are we going to,
get our tuxes tomorrow or what?"

"Yeah, give me call, we'll hook up."

"Alright then, I gotta go to work, later."

Heinz starts his car.

"Late."

Zeus starts his car and they both leave, Zeus heads home. It's now evening, Zeus is watching TV and the phone rings, he picks up the phone.

"Hello?"

It's his father, Socrates. Socrates is a proud Greek Man, who is living his "American Dream," His word is law and never questioned, has been on Zeus to choose a college. Zeus, however, remains uncertain of what he wants to do with his life. This is a constant issue between the two.

"Ti knaneis."

"Eh, watching TV."

"Echeis scholiki douleia?"

"Nope!"

Zeus bites his lip. Instantly Zeus knows he should have told his dad that he had schoolwork to finish.

"Ummm, what's up?"

"Echasa to plyntirio piaton mou."

Zeus gives an *"Oh Shit"* look.

"And?"

"Do I have to translate?

*"I need you to come up here
and wash dishes."*

"Pop, why me all the time?"

"Giati, giati, giati?"

Zeus holds the phone away from his ear. Socrates is
pissed off and he looks like he's about to explode. He now
speaks to Zeus in English, to voice his displeasure of his
son's constant questions.

*"When my father wanted something, I helped,
No questions asked. I work hard to give you nice
clothes, to put food on the table and have a roof
over your head. I give you things I never had when
I was a boy! Your father now needs your help, and
this is how you treat me? You ask why? Listen carefully,
put down the remote, get off your ass and get up here
now, I'm running low on clean dishes."*

Zeus looks at his watch. It's 7 o'clock.

"Ok."

"Hmmp! Yamoto keratosou, malaka!"

Socrates hangs up the phone, exasperated with this son, gives a Ralph Kramden, "Bang, Zoom" motion with his hand showing five fingers.

Zeus gets up off the couch in the living room, walks out the front door of his house, walks down the steps onto the driveway and up to his car. He has difficulty turning it over, but it finally starts. He heads off to his father's restaurant, "The Mountainhome Diner". Zeus drives past many sites along Stroudsburg. He if forced to slow down due to honeymooners crossing the highway. Later, he runs into tourists who are observing the lush green along the highway. He notices the fifty mile per hour sign and looks down at his speedometer, which shows 35 mph. Zeus beeps his horn several times.

"Tourists, move it."

Zeus crosses the double line on a blind curve. The car ahead of him blows his horn. Zeus passes the old couple in their car and promptly gives them five fingers upon hearing the horn. This Greek gesture is worse than flipping someone the bird.

"Gámisé ."

We see Zeus' Pinto pulling into the parking lot in the rear of the building. Zeus steps out of the car and passes by his uncle, Sotiri, who is dragging a trash can towards the dumpster.

"Geia sou Día, brávo sou,
írthes na mas voithíseis!"

"Yeah, the Diner's Dish Bitch is here."

Zeus walks into the kitchen and sees his dad and gives him a wave. Walks over to a box, grabs an apron, and puts it on. He then walks over to the place where the dishwasher works to wash dishes. The dishes are piled high. He grabs the top dishes, which are full of food, and starts cleaning the food off the dishes into the special rubber hole, which empties into a trash can. Unfortunately, the trash can was being emptied by Sotiri, so the food, falls through the hole and splatters on to the floor, getting Zeus' sneakers all messed up.

*"Shit! I'll take some chicken with gravy
and a side order of Nike's please."*

"Psst, tha to chreiasteís aftó."

Sotiri hands Zeus the trash can.

"Thanks!"

New waitress Sheila walks in and adds more dishes to the table, which is overflowing. She looks at Zeus, smiles, Zeus notices her too.

"Hi!"

"Hi!"

Zeus puts the trash can in its place. Sheila walks out of the kitchen.

"Where are the rags?"

"Brostá"

"Thanks."

Zeus walks up to the front doors, which open up to the front of the diner and looks around. He sees a lot of activity in the diner. People are sitting at the counter eating, all booths are full of people eating, and waitresses are running around working. He steps back and walks over to the side door and notices his father, who is busy fixing orders. He looks out the side view and notices that the dining room is empty. He walks over and sees two waitresses chatting it up and finishing up their conversation. Sally, 50's, a tough old bird, who has worked at the diner since it open, smiles at her guy, Zeus.

"Ladies."

"Zeus, how's my favorite guy?"
I'm okay. I'm looking for
a rag, you got one."

Sally looks and finds a rag.

"Oh, here's one."

Sally throws it over to Zeus.

"Thanks.

Zeus notices a new waitress and makes eye contact. She is smiling at Zeus.

"Hi, I'm Zeus. My friends call me Z."

"Oh, I'm sorry, Z, this is Sheila.
Sheila, this is the boss's son. Z
is the standby dishwasher."

Sheila extends her hand and shakes Zeus' hand. Zeus sits down next to Sally across from Sheila.

"Nice to officially meet you."

"Nice to meet you too."

*"So, was that you, your dad
was yelling at on the phone?"*

"Yeah, you know how parents are."

"Does he always yell at you like that?"

*"Yeah, but you have to understand where my
dad came from. He grew up in Greece, didn't
have any telephones, no running water, no
toilets, just an outhouse. Heck, if they needed
water they got it from a well. So, if they needed
to communicate, they'd yelled."*

Zeus' dad walks out of the kitchen into the dining room
walking towards Zeus.

"Psst."

Zeus looks up notices his dad and gets up and holds up the
rag he used on his Nike's.

*"We didn't have any rags in the kitchen,
I had to get one from out here."*

"We're running low on clean dishes."

"Okay, okay."

Zeus then turns and responds to Sheila.

"Nice meeting you, Sheila."

Sheila smiles. Zeus gets up and walks towards the kitchen. Sally sticks up for Zeus with Socrates.

*"Soc, you're too hard on Zeus. You
need to give the kid a break."*

*"Break? What break? My father never
gave me a break and look how I turned out."*

"A cranky old fart."

"Yes, but a rich cranky old fart!

Soc laughs, Sally shakes her head in disbelief.

*"Listen, when I was Zeus' age, I worked
for my father full-time and didn't have the
chance to go to school and follow my dreams,
I worked because I had too, because my family
needed me. Zeus, he's smart boy, he can be
anything he wants to be. Straight a's in school,
but he has no ambition, no drive."*

*"Soc, this side of the world is a
completely different place to grow
up in, especially today."*

*"It's not different. Same
shovel, just different piles."*

Sally shakes her head

*"There's no reasoning
with you Socrates."*

"Look, if I'm tough on Zeus, it's because I love him
and want him to succeed. Tough times don't last, tough
people do. I just want Zeus to be ready for the world.

"You know, for only having a 3rd
grade education, you're pretty smart."

"Eh, some people they just learn quicker than
others. Soc smiles, sally shakes her head."
"Okay, now back work."

Chapter Two -I Can Jump You

Several hours go by and we see Zeus cleaning, sweeping, and mopping the dinner, scrubbing toilets, and cleaning up every dish that was on the drop off table. Zeus sprays water on the pickup table and squeegees it dry, puts dishes in the dishwasher and turns the machine on. Moments later, Sheila comes in and puts more dishes on the drop off table.

"What's this?"

*"Sorry, there was one table in the back
that didn't get cleared off, sorry."*

"No biggie, don't sweat it."

Sheila smiles, Zeus smiles back. She walks out of the kitchen to the front of the diner. Zeus raises his eyebrows. Sotiri walks up to him, he has his coat on and is ready to leave.

*"An théleis boreís na tis
to dóseis apópse!"*

Sotiri makes a motion with his fist back and forth, Zeus smiles. Sheila walks into the kitchen with even more dirty dishes. Sotiri leaves.

"Sorry, I missed these too."

Uncle Sotiri continues to speak in Greek, talking up his nephew.

"Z, To vlépo sta mátia tis!"

Zeus turns to look at Sotiri. Sotiri is making the fist motion back and forth again. Zeus turns and talks to Sheila and starts shaking his head, jokingly.

"Sheila, Sheila Sheila, What
am I going to do with you?"

"Sorry. I know you want
to get out of here."

"Well, maybe you'll make
it up to me one day."

"Well, there's a party my
Sorority tonight? Want to go?"

"Cool."

Sheila is smiling from ear to ear as is Zeus. She's beaming and walks out back.

Some twenty-five minutes later, we see interior lights being turned off. Zeus' father hits the code on the burglar alarm, then both Zeus and his father walk out of the diner to his father's car.

"Good night, pops."

"You want me to wait to make
sure that car of yours starts?"

"Nah, I'll be alright, besides Sheila's
still here if I've got a problem."

Socrates looks over the Sheila's car, rolls his eyes and shakes his head.

*"I don't be too late, your
mother will worry."*

"I know, I know, good night."

Zeus starts his car and drives over to Sheila's car. Both cars are parked facing headlights to headlights. Her hood is up, and she's bent overlooking under the hood with a flashlight. She has a nice ass. Zeus has an inner monolog going on, Talk about bootylious. I certainly hope destiny allows this child to jump start that tonight. Zeus turns off his ignition and gets out of his car.

"Hey, what's up?"

*"Oh, my car has been acting up and
not running right. I was hoping it would
get me home tonight, but it won't start."*

"Where do you live?"

"East Stroudsburg."

*"You're a long way from home. Let me
look at it. If I can't fix it, I'll give you a ride.
Can I see your flashlight?"*

Zeus looks around the motor with the flashlight. Zeus looks at the motor and see's that the spark plug wire is frayed.

*"Looks like your spark plug wire is
frayed. Was the car, throbbing like
this on the way up here?"*

Zeus makes fist motion similar to what Sotiri was making earlier.

"Yeah."

*"Well, that's probably
your problem."*

Zeus gets out his wallet, opens it, and gets out a Band-Aid.

*"You always carry band-aids
in your wallet?"*

*"One thing my dad taught me,
always carry a band-aid with you
cause the first aid kit is always empty."*

Zeus wraps up the wire and shuts the hood.

"Keys?"

*"In the ignition. If you get it started
I'll owe you big time."*

"Yes, yes, you will!"

Zeus and Sheila get in the car, Zeus on the driver's side, Sheila in the passenger's seat. Zeus starts up the car, he rev's it up. It sounds great.

"You're the man!"

"Let's celebrate."

Zeus goes to turn on the radio.

"It's broken."

"Cassette work?"

Sheila shakes her head.

"Nope."

"Why such a long face?"

Zeus pulls out two cold beers out of his pockets.

"Here, let me see that smile again."

"Whoa!"

Zeus hands Sheila a beer. They both twist off the tops, clink their beers in celebration and drink. Zeus takes a few swigs off his beer, Sheila chugs hers.

"Corona, that's my favorite brew!

"You get these out of your wallet too?"

"No, my dad keeps a stash in the walk in."

"Sally was right. You are sweet."

Their eyes meet and they kiss. Their kiss turns into an extended, passionate kiss. We see a clock in her car. It says 11:07. A Police car enters parking lot. Moments later, the Officer tilts his head to one side as he's looking at the cars in the parking lot. They consist of Sheila's and Zeus's cars. The officer gets out of his squad car with a flashlight in hand. He approaches Sheila's car. The windows are fogged up; he turns and walks to Zeus's car. He flashes his flashlight into Zeus's car. No sign of Zeus. He turns around, looks at Sheila's car, then proceeds back to his squad car and gets onto his cell phone. Sheila and Zeus are still making out. Sheila's blouse is unzipped. Zeus' shirt is off.

"Have you got coverage?"

"Yeah, but I fixed your car. Why?"

"No, I don't mean auto coverage."

Makes a gesture like, you know, a condom.

"I mean, do you have coverage?"
*"Oh coverage? Yeah, sure
where's my wallet?"*

*"I think it's actually
under my butt."*

She lifts up and there's Zeus's wallet. Zeus starts fumbling through his wallet to find a condom.

"I know. I've got one in here."

Zeus cannot locate it.

"Hang on, I know I've got one in here."

Zeus continues to look but cannot find one. He looks at Sheila, defeated.

*"Sorry Z, no glove, no love.
Maybe it wasn't meant to be."*

*"No, no, no it is, it is meant to be,
I'm sure I've got one in my car.*

"I'll be right back."

Zeus opens Sheila's car door and bolts half naked to his car. We follow Zeus fumbling through his backpack looking for a rubber.

"Coverage, coverage, we need coverage."

Sheila is trying to watch Zeus but can't be of the fogged windows of the back seat. She hears a tap on the driver's side window.

"Come on in, I'm ready."

The door opens and Sheila lets out a scream. Instead of Zeus, we see Socrates. Sheila screams yet again. Zeus hears the scream. He bumps his head as he gets out of the car to run to Sheila's aid. The diner's parking lot is dimly lit and as Z approaches Sheila, he stops dead in his tracks, as he sees his dad outside Sheila's car door.

"Pop, what are you doing here?"

"Officer Johnson called me and told me that the new girl was having trouble getting her car started."

Zeus is speechless. We hear Sheila's car start up and peel out. Sheila car lights light up Zeus's half naked body. Zeus gets a why me look on his face. It now dons upon Socrates that his son is half naked in his parking lot.

"What are you doing half naked in my parking lot?"

Chapter Three—Do I Look Chinese

Papadakis home in afternoon, Zeus's Mother, Alexia, is in the kitchen cooking. Alexia is an average-looking woman, who believes family is everything and has devoted her life to make sure that her family is happy and healthy. The phone rings.

"Hello? Yes. Zeus! Telephone!"

Zeus picks up the phone in his room.

"Ma, I got it. Hello?"

Zeus's best friend, Heinz, is on the line.

"Pós ta pas jerkoff."

*"Did you just call me a Jerkoff in Greek?
Put down the Google Translator and
come and pick me up already."*

*"I've been at home waiting for your
sorry ass. I thought you were going to
pick me up so we can get our tuxes."*

"No, I drove last time, Vlaka!"

*"Hey, did you just call
me an asshole?"*

"No, I called you stupid, Kólos."

"Wait, did you just call an asshole Vlaka?"

*"Now you're really learning Heinzy, so drop
Google Translator to a real Greek Translator."*

*"Ass, grass or gas, nobody
rides for free, translate that."*

*"Just get your ass over
here and pick me up.*

Moments later, Zeus walks into the kitchen and smells his mother's cooking. Zeus' dad is sitting at the table reading a Greek Newspaper, smoking a cigarette, while Zeus's mother is cooking.

"Zeus. Want some Spaticho?"

Zeus is eating feta cheese and bread.

*"Ma, I'm 18. In a few days, I'm graduating.
from high school. I'm ready for a change.
How about some Chinese? You should make
some fried rice! I had some in home-ec class, it
annihilates. Come to think of it, I bet you this
feta would go great with some fried rice."*

*"Zeus, do I look Chinese? No, I'm Greek. I make
Greek food. You want Chinese, go to Danny Woo's."*

A car pulls in, we hear a car horn. Zeus starts heading out Heinz to get their tuxedos.

"That's my cue!"

"Perímene!"

Socrates grabs Zeus's hand. Zeus sits back down. Zeus is not happy, because he knows the conversation that is going to take place. It's about which College he will attend. The problem is that Zeus is uncertain about his future.

"What?"

Socrates is trying to meet his son halfway by speaking to him in English. Education for his two boys is paramount to him.

"Which college are you attending?"

*"Can't we do this next week after
the graduation and the prom?"*

"Ochi tóra!"

Socrates slams his hand on the table, angered by son's response and lack of urgency. He also goes back to his native tongue of Greek.

*"I can't now, Pop. I've got
to get my tux for the prom."*

"Póte tin epómeni evdomáda?"

Zeus just sits there with a stern look on his face. He's been putting off choosing a college.

"Yeah Pop, next week, I promise."

Zeus's procrastination of the subject irritates Socrates to no end. He doesn't understand his son's indecisive attitude. Once again, Socrates' voice goes from soft to loud.

*"Next week! Everybody else has
picked a college. Why do you wait?"*

We hear Heinz's car horn blowing a real long time.

*"I don't know, pop. Can I go, Heinz and
I have to get our Tuxes for graduation."*

*"I never had the chance to go
to college. You have to go!"*

Socrates bangs his fist on the table again. Alexis as usual is trying to defuse the situation.

*"Take it easy Socrates, it's not
good for your blood pressure."*

*"Pop, relax. We'll talk about it next week, let
me enjoy graduation and my prom and then
we'll sit down and talk about it, okay?"*

"Okay next week, you chose, no accuses."

Socrates sighs. Zeus stands up, then Socrates stands up.

"And next week, you think with your head."

Socrates taps on Zeus's forehead and then grabs Zeus's crotch. Zeus is shocked, embarrassed, and speechless. Zeus's mother is horrified.

"Socrates!"

He releases his son's manhood and lets out an ultimatum to his eldest son.

*"If you don't go to college, you'll be
working full time at the diner."*

Zeus, bewildered, looks at his mom and leaves running out of the house.

We hear Zeus's mother and father argue as he runs down the driveway. He gets in Heinz's car.

*"Hey, what took you so long? Let me
guess, you were, avnanismós?"*

Makes a jerking off gesture.

"Dude, my dad just grabbed my package."

"What?"

"No joke."

"Your dad just grabbed your dick."

*"Yeah. Let's get out of here,
I'm completely weirded out."*

*"Hey, if that's something you Greek guys are
into, I don't think I want any more lessons."*

Heinz starts the car, starts driving down the street. Meanwhile, in the house, Alexis is sticking up for her son.

*"Never embarrass our son like that
again. You think you're back in Samos?"*

Socrates lights up a cigarette.

"Entáxei, stamáta na paraponiésai."

"He's your son, not an animal on the farm."

"Ti sto diáolo, tha stamatíseis!"

Socrates bangs his hand on the table. The phone rings. Alexis, frustrated by her husband, answers it.

"Hello? Oh Dimitri, how are you? Oh? Let me let you talk with Socrates. Socrates! Telephone, it's Dimitri."

"Ti thelei? Megáli páfsi."

"To wish you a happy birthday."

"It's not my birthday!"

"Okay, then you find out."

She hands him the phone. Socrates has a pensive look.

"What do you want!"

Dimitri Papadakis, Socrates' youngest brother, his charm and always gotten him by in life. Socrates resents him, since it is Socrates who is always having to bail his brother out. Dimitri manages a resort diner that Socrates owns. It's located in North Carolina, the Outer Banks. Dimitri also has a gambling addiction. He's just lost two grand, but he knows in his bones that his luck is about to change. There is a man in the sitting on a chair and another huge guy with a bat.

"Whoa. I just called to tell you how well the Diner is doing. You were right when you said, The Banks, that's the place to have a diner."

"You should listen to your brother. Work hard and I'll sell you it to you one day. Now I know you didn't call to flatter me. How much?"

*"I am working hard Soc and that will be
a great honor. I'm not going to lie to you. I
do need some money. My eh, meat supplier, he
eh, he went belly up and..."*

*"That's good, that means you should be
able to get a good deal on your meats,
because he must liquidate his assets."*

*"Yeah, that's exactly why I'm calling. I need
three grand to be able to get this great deal."*

"You need money? Call the bank."

*"See, that's just it. Today's Thursday, it'll take the
bank at least until Monday to process the loan."*

The guy with the bat in the background is tapping the bat in his hand impatiently.

*"And then that'll be too late. He'll
have sold it to another restaurant."*

*"Fine, I will put the money in
the diner account tomorrow."*

*"Could you, money gram it to me instead? That
would be to Flair's Pharmacy, and I'll pick the
money up there. It's got to be right now, though.
He's got someone that's willing to pay $2700
Cash. Yeah, F-l-a-i-r-'-s Pharmacy. Thanks and
once again, our customers thank you too."*

We hear dial tone.

"Okay, love you, brother. Bye."

Dimitri hangs up the phone.

"Okay, the money is on its way. We're all good. In fact, I had my brother send an extra grand, so I could play while we wait for the money."

The man in charge of the Poker game has overheard Dimitri's hustle to Socrates and didn't like what he heard.

"No, you're cut off, that's it, no more."

"What are you talking about? I got you your money, and I've got more cash on the way."

"Sorry, you're banned. This was your swan song."

"What's the deal? Do people gamble here or what? Since when did you get a conscience?"

Gambling guy now has ball bat in his hand and points it to his chest.

"My house, my cards, my rules, your brother probably works really hard for that money your about to screw him out of, so no more. Now go with Kyle, get my money and don't ever come back."

Chapter Four—No Sex In My Car:

Both Heinz and Zeus are at Sal's Tux and Tails. The two are behind dressing room doors. They open at once both are dressed in their tuxes. Heinz is grilling Zeus about Zeus's prom date Denise.

"So, what's the deal with Denise?"

"I'm taking her to the prom."

"And?"

Drawn out.

"What?"

Confused.

*"How many times have
you gone out with her?"*

"Are you writing a book?"

*"Dude, that girl is fine! What's she
doing with a shmoe like you."*
*"She's probably been watching me
showering the guy's locker room."*

"Yeah, whatever Mr. Delusional."
*"I mean, I've got to measure the thing
with a yardstick, instead of a ruler."*

*"Z, guys don't talk to other guys
about the size of their…"*

Zeus shakes his head."

"Yeah, I guess you're right."

"Oh course I'm right. Do you think chicks talk to each other about the size of their tits? No! Wait a minute, I'm getting a vision of chicks comparing each other's tits. Oh, there's Denise's pair, their perfect. I can't believe you're gonna see her rack."

"Yeah, too bad the old man isn't going to see the size of them."

Makes motion of big breasts. Heinz shakes his head in disbelief. The boys finish up with their tuxedos and head to the local Vinyl Shop.

"Why do you do that?"

"What?"

"You're always thinking about what your dad will think or what your dad will say."

"I don't know, I just need his respect, his blessing. I can't explain it. I wish he'd just get off my back about college."

"Hey about the college thing, just go to your old man's alma mater, that's what I'm doing. Once I said that, he just left my shit alone. He's all proud, chest puffed out, that's my boy."

"Coward's way out."

*"Maybe, but I've got my summer free to get
faded and wax it and my dad's not grabbing
my dick about going to college."*

"I'm screwed. My dad didn't go to college."

*"Yeah, but at least you'll have an opportunity to
see Denise's sweater puppies. Heck, I might even
let your dad grab my package, for a chance to
see Denise's personal floatation devices."*

"You're sick and I don't mean that in a good way."

Hours later, Zeus's bathroom, evening. Zeus is getting ready for the Prom, shaving, applying underarm deodorant, making muscles in the mirror. He then moves to the bedroom where he combs his hair, puts on his shirt, pants socks and finally fixing his tie. There is a knock on his door. Alexis answers the door.

"Zeus, Heinz is here."

"Okay!"

Zeus opens his bedroom door. Zeus mother gets all emotional.

*"Oh, look at my boy. You
look like a movie star."*

She straightens his tie, then flicks some lint from his tuxedo and gives him a kiss

"Thanks Ma."

We hear Socrates.

*"Does the movie star know where
what college he's going to."*

Zeus shakes his head in disbelief as he walks down the hall and down the steps. His mother follows.

*"Don't worry about your father. You enjoy your
big night. You celebrate, you have a good time,
don't worry about college, it will still be there
tomorrow."*

Zeus hugs his mother tighter with her reassurance, then releases her.

"Thanks ma, you always know what to say."

They proceed to walk to the living room. Where Socrates and Heinz are situated. Socrates is reading the
paper.

*"Socrates, look at Zeus.
Doesn't he look handsome?"*

Socrates veers his head around the Greek newspaper, with reading glasses on the end of his nose

"You have prophylactics."

"Socrates!"

*"What? It's the boy's prom, you
think he's going to bowling?"*

Heinz is snickering, Zeus kind of laughs. Ma gets a look on her face like, very funny, you won't be getting some for a while. Ma calls for Adonis, Zeus's preteen brother.

"Adonis, come and look at your brother."

*"Ma, we've got to go. Pops can
I have the keys to the car."*

*"Wait, I almost forgot to take
a picture of you and Heinz."*

Ma runs to the kitchen to get her camera. Socrates
puts down the newspaper. He has a stern look on his face.

*"No drink, no drive. You fill up the
car when you bring it back, but most
important, no sex in my car."*

*"Socrates! Okay, you two boys
stand together. Okay say, cheese."*
*"Ma, we really got to get going,
I've still got to pick up my date."*

"Do it for your mother, say cheese!"

Socrates gives Zeus the keys and goes back to reading your
paper. Socrates throws Zeus the keys to the car.

"You remember, no sex in my car!"

Socrates proceeds back to reading his paper. Ma walks Heinz
and Zeus to the door. Heinz and Zeus start to leave the house.

"Zeus."

Zeus turns around.

"Yeah, Ma?"

"Come here."

Zeus walks back to his mother.

"Yeah."

Ma hugs him, then kisses his cheek and hands him a hundred-dollar bill.

"Here, you have a good time."

Zeus looks and sees that is a hundred-dollar bill and hugs her again.

"Ma, you're the best."

"Have a good time."

"Okay."

Zeus is now walking away towards his father's car.

"You tell me all about it tomorrow."

"Alright."

Zeus has unlocked the car doors. Heinz gets in and Zeus finishes his conversation with his mother.

"And Zeus."

"Yeah, Ma."

"No sex in your father's car."

Zeus and Heinz laugh. The boys are cruising through Stroudsburg thinking they are the shit on their way to pick up Zeus's date, Denise.

"No sex in the car, where
did that come from?"

"I had a situation with one of the
waitresses a few nights ago."

"Where?"

"Behind my Dad's Diner."

"Behind, your dad's dinner
is the parking lot."

"Yeah."
"What is it with you and parking lots?"

"I don't plan these things they
just happen. Subject changes."

"So tell me again, why not going to
the prom with a date. Is the way to go?"

"Bro, how many times do I have to tell
you. Check it, the prom is supposed to
be one of those once in a lifetime events
in a girl's life. Right?"

Zeus nods his head in agreement.

"So I've done a little research."

Zeus now shakes his head as to say, "Here we go".

"Go ahead Professor."

"Thank you. Young ladies have been waiting four years for this night. It's a night that they feel the need to be less inhibited. They feel the sense that the world now sees them as adults."

Zeus pretending to be enthralled in Heinz's theory.

"Um hum, go ahead."

Makes the jerk off motion with his hand.

"They feel the need to."

Zeus interrupts.

"Lose their virginity? To bone their brains out, to take a ride on the baloney pony."

"B-i-n-g-o! And you still a virgin?"

"True, but at least I didn't have to join the 4-h club to lose my mine."

"Oh, that's low, that's baaad."

Zeus is in disbelief.

"I'm supposed to be taking romance tips from bozo panarian."

"Bozo what?"

"If you have to ask."

Heinz cuts him off.

*"Whatever. I'm just saying that there will
be more tang tonight at the prom, then when
the astronauts landed on the moon."*

This triggers something in Heinz. He pulls out two cigars and hands one to Zeus.

"Right on!"

Heinz starts to light up.

"What are you doing?"

"I'm going to smoke a cigar."

"Not in my dad's car."

*"Z, the old man didn't say anything
about smoking a stogie in his ride, he
just said, "don't have sex".*

*"Trust me, pops doesn't want us
smoking cigars in his car."*

*"You're kidding me, right? Your dad smokes
more than a lone vibrator at a lesbian orgy."*

Zeus ponders Heinz' analogy.

"Yeah, I guess you're right."

They both fire up their cigars and are just cruising.

"Dude, we're hella tight."

"Yeah, we are."

They arrive at Denise's house.

"I'll be right back."

Zeus runs up to Denise's door, rings the doorbell. Denise's dad answers the door.

"Can I help you?"

"Yeah, I'm here to pick up Denise."

"Denise?"

"Yeah?"

"Just a second."

Turns away from Zeus and yells.

"Wanda!"

Zeus is confused. Suddenly Denise's mother, Wanda, appears at the door.

*"Wanda, this is Zeus, he's here to
pick up Denise for the prom."*

Denise's mother looks uncomfortable. She smiles, the father shakes his head and leaves.

"Zeus, it's a pleasure to meet you.

"Didn't Denise get a hold of you?"

"No?"

*"Oh well, she's already
left for the prom."*

"Already left?"

*"Yeah. I think she had to help out last
minute with some decorations or
something. Didn't she call you?"*

"No."

"Well, she's at the prom."

"Okay... Well, it was nice meeting you."

"Oh, you too, hon."

Fake smile plaster on her face.

"Bye."

The door closes. Zeus is just standing at the door dumfounded. Heinz honks the horn and breaks Zeus from his trance. Zeus walks back to the car, gets in and receives the inquisition from Heinz.

"Dude, so where's the rack?"

Zeus, still looking bewildered, answers.

"At the prom, working on decorations."

*"I didn't know she was on the
Committee. She's not."*

Zeus starts the car and leaves for the prom. There is complete silence between Zeus and Heinz until they roll up on the prom. Zeus parks his dad's car; they get out and are walking towards the prom.

*"Maybe, somebody called
her last minute to help."*

Zeus's mind is elsewhere. He is almost obvious to Heinz's commentary.

"Yeah, I bet that's what happened."

Zeus is still thinking about it. They get to registration and suddenly everyone is whispering at pointing at Zeus and Heinz.

*"See, what'd I tell you, all the cheek a's
are digging our machismo."*

"I'm going to find Denise."

*"Go ahead, I catch up. I need to scout the
available talent for my next home video."*

Zeus smiles.

"Yeah, whatever Francis Ford cop-a-feel."

Heinz disappears into a sea of people looking for his next victim. Zeus goes searching for Denise. Zeus finally spots her. She is standing talking with a sailor and another girl.

"Denise!"

"Zeus?

"I thought i was supposed to pick you up."

*"I'm sorry I forgot to call you. Zeus, this
is my friend, Mike? He's home on leave
from the Navy."*

They shake hands. Zeus looks a little numb.

*"Yeah, didn't you graduate
a couple of years ago?"*

*"Yeah, I've been overseas, but when
my cousin over here wrote and said..."*

Points to the other girl there.

*"She didn't have a date to the prom. I
decided it would be nice if i took her.
It's a once in a lifetime thing you know."*

*"Yeah, that's what I keep hearing.
Excuse me for a second."*

Zeus is figuring out something is going on. He steps
backwards a few steps and hears Heinz in the background,
which gets his attention. Heinz shows up with a gal on each arm.

"What it be Lee?"

Heinz turns around and looks at Mike and Denise.

"Is that Denise?"

"Yeah."

"Should have followed my advice on the pie, bro."

Mike kisses Denise. Zeus can't believe his eyes. Zeus loses it and sprints through the dance floor at Mike.

"Oh shit, Houston we've
got a big ass problem."

Heinz takes off after Zeus, leaving both of his girls behind. Zeus grabs the sailor and pulls him away from the kiss. The two go crashing to the ground.

"What the fuck!"

Denise's date flips over and push Zeus off.

"What's your problem, asshole?"

"I don't know. Maybe the fact
that you're with my date."

"Look, I don't think you get the deal."

"I guess I don't."

"You're a replacement date. I came
home to take my girlfriend to her Senior
Prom. So if you don't like it, tough shit.
You want some? Come get some."

Denise backs away, sensing the impending fisticuffs. Zeus just glares at Mike. Mike provokes Zeus.

"Yeah, just as I thought, no sack."

"Why don't you just toss my Greek Salad?"

"What?"

*"You heard me! Why don't you
just toss my Greek salad."*

Makes a suck it motion to his crotch Mike becomes enraged. Mike charges Zeus, dropping both of them to the ground, where they wrestle around, punches are thrown. A crowd gathers around as they fight. Finally, a chaperone comes in to break up the fight. Both Zeus and mike are being held my students. Denise is on Mike's side.

"What's going on here?"

*"I'll tell what's going on here, that
squid is being an octopus with my date."*

Zeus points towards Mike, the Chaperone looks at Mike.

*"I don't know what he's talking about, sir. Denise and I
have been seeing each other for over a year and a half. I'm
on leave from the Navy, so I could take my girl to her
senior prom and this guy bum rushes me from behind. I
was just protecting myself and my date."*

*"Look, Zeus, you're a good kid and I like you, but I think
your actions tonight warrant you leaving the prom."*

*"Leave? Me? No! I paid my money,
I've got the tux, let the squid walk."*

*"I think by the tone of your voice, you're
obviously, the cause of the trouble here.*

Now I'm going to ask you nicely once again. Leave before I call the authorities."

"Bye, bye."

Mike waves bye to Zeus. Zeus starts to go after Mike. Heinz holds him back.

"Mrs. Crowley call 911."

Heinz interjects.

"No need for the po, we're out Audi."

Heinz pulls Zeus away. Zeus is reluctantly going, the crowd is slowly dissipating, they make it out to the parking lot. Heinz is trying to reason with Zeus to let him have the keys to Zeus's dad's car.

"Dude, you are in no condition to drive."

"I'm alright to drive."

"Z, you just attacked a fuckin' marine, have been threatened to have the cops called on you, you're not driving."

"Fine, you drive."

Zeus throws his dad's keys to Heinz. They both get into Zeus's dad's car and leave. They go past a jeep that has a bumper sticker on it that says, "The size of the boat does matter."

"Stop!"

"Why?"

"Just back the car up."

Heinz stops, puts Socrates in reverse.

"Yeah, see that."

"What?"

"The bumper sticker."

*"The size of the boat
does matter. Yeah, so."*

"I bet you it's that Navy prick's ride."

"A chance to even the score."

"Yup, yup."

Zeus reaches into his dad's glove box and pulls out a can of shoe polish.

"What are you going to do with that?"

"Follow the master."

Zeus gets out of the car and lines Mike's windshield wipers with shoe polish, then sets the windshield wipers up so that they'll go on when mike starts the car.

"What's with you and windshield wipers?"

Zeus smiles.

*"Trust me, this is something
he'll never forget."*

*"Zeus, the thinker. Me, I'd
have just done this."*

Heinz jumps up onto Mike's Jeep, he unzips his zipper and starts peeing on Mike's front seats.

*"A little less subtle, but
effective none the less."*

Chapter Five—Chin Chin Checkers

Heinz, wanting to save the big night, takes Zeus to a college bar that serves him.

"Where are we going?"

"Trust me."

"Famous last words."

Heinz is lightly hurt by Zeus's word. He pulls over the Cadillac.

"Are you my best friend?

Zeus nods his "Yes."

*"Then trust me, I've got a plan that
will blow away that shit show of a
Prom. You with me?"*

"Yeah, I'm just still pissed."

*"Don't be, I promise. Tonight will be a
night to remember. How's your liver?"*

Zeus thinks about it, smiles, and speaks

"Hells Yes, let's do this."

The two head to Heinz's surprise location. The two finally pull off the highway and head into a College Bar called "Tesla's Tavern" and head up to the front door, which is fashioned after an old fashion speakeasy. You need to answer a question regarding Nikola Tesla.

"What is this place?"

"Tesla's Tavern, Heaven on Earth."

"But I don't have a fake ID like you."

"Bro, all you need is a knowledge of Tesla."

Zeus is confused by the premise of a bar that revolves around Nikola Tesla. The boys walk up to the front door, which is an old fashion prohibition door with a peephole. Heinz knocks on the door and a pair of eyes peer through. The man recognizes Heinz.

"Hey Heinz."

The man's eyes move to Zeus.

"Who's your friend?"

Heinz's acknowledges Zeus.

"This is my boy, Zeus."

"How are you doing, Zeus?"

"I'm good."

Heinz wants to get in.

"Hit me with a question."

The doorman looks at both young men and speaks.

"You each get one question, one shot, one opportunity, so don't blow it, understand?"

"I got you, Slim Shady. Hit me."

"What type of alcohol did Tesla drink?"

Zeus gets a concerned look on his face. Sure, he knows some basic Tesla, but what type of alcohol does he drink? "Fuck Me" and how does Heinz know? Heinz looks at Zeus like, I totally got this.

"Scotch Whiskey"

The man's eyes shift to Zeus.

"What distiller?"

Zeus's mind is short circuiting, distiller? If ever the term "A deer in the headlights" was applicable, it was Zeus. It was now. The doorman senses the term distiller has thrown Zeus.

"Brand, what type of Scotch whiskey?"

Zeus closes his eyes and scans his dad's alcohol inventory to see if he can see the label, shit no Scotch Whiskey.

"We're kind of running a here son,
so if you don't know, you got to go."

Zeus acknowledges the doorman.

"Let me check one more place."

Zeus uses his photographic memory to scour his local liquor store. Ah, there it is, the Whiskey's. Scotch Whiskey's where are they? There they are, "Shit" more than one, Glenlivet 12 Year, Dewar's 15 year Glenlivet 12 year. Fuck, which one?"

"Dewar's."

The man at the door just stares at Zeus and then Heinz, then nods his head affirmatively and lets the two new graduates in.

"Enjoy gentlemen."

The boys acknowledge the statement, nod their heads and head into the Tavern. The Tavern is filled with a mix of college kids and a few older individuals. The bartender sees Heinz and Z walk in; he nods to them. A girl yells at Heinz and then walks up to him. A guy walks away with his dozen mini bottles of tequila.

"Heinzzy!!! Nice threads."

*"Thanks Bev, yeah, I'm
stone cold pippin, huh?"*

"You look really good."

"Good enough to get lucky?"

*"No, but good enough for
me to buy you a beer."*

Beverly turns to the bartender and places an order.

"Can I have heiny for my friend Heinzy and..."

She looks to Z.

"What do you want Z?"

*"I'll take a hinny too. (Mumbles
under his breath, "Yours.")."*

The Beverly smiles.

"Make that three Heinekens."

Heinz and Z share a laugh, then Heinz reassures Zeus that the night will be a night to remember.

"Man, screw the prom, this night
is going to rock, it's gonna be just."

Zeus and Heinz's finish sentence in unison.

"Too sweet!"

They punch fists. The College gal pays for the beers, then turns around and hands Heinz and Zeus a beer.

"What was that all about?"

Zeus answers Bev's question.

"Nothing! We're just happy that
you bought us drinks! Thanks!"

"You're welcome, come on."

All three walk into the main portion of the bar, which consists of five tables with four chairs each. Each table has a board game design on it, similar to a board game used for checkers or chess. In the corner, there is a jukebox playing music. There are people chatting, drinking their beers out of the bottles. The bar is packed everyone looks they are in college. There is a group of girls talking when they suddenly recognize Heinz and then the entire Tavern acknowledges Heinz.

"Heennnzzzzzyyyyyyyyyy!"

*"People! Thank you, thank you very much, no
Applause just bra's, panties, and dorm keys."*

A huge pair of men's underwear come flying at Heinz.

"Dudes, need not apply."

Z comes upon a unique game being played. We see an Asian girl sitting at the table, playing a board game with a guy. We see what looks like a game of checkers being readied to be played however instead of plastic pieces, we see bottles of Tequila and Jack Daniels being set up in place of the pieces. A former classmate, Mark, approaches Zeus.

*"Hey Z, what's up with
you and Heinz in tuxes?"*

"Don't even ask."

"Wasn't it you guy's prom tonight?"

"Man, f the prom, we're here to get faded."

Zeus and Mark raise his beers in a toast. Mark follows up a final courtesy question.

"So, what else is up?"

"Ssdp."

"Ssdp?"

"Same shovel, different pile."

They both laugh. Z sees a game of checkers being played. The game is now over, and the girl gets up to go to the bathroom, the guy gets up to buy more booze.

"What are they playing?

"Chin Chin Checkers.

"With those little bottles?"

*"Yeah, it's pretty wild when you jump
the other person's piece, you get to keep
the bottle or drink it."*

"I've never seen that game played that before."

*"I've played it a couple of times, but i lost.
A set of bottles is about 20 bucks, so now
I stick to pool, get it stick to pool."*

"Don't quit your day job."

Heinz makes his way over to Zeus to see how he's doing.

"How's it growing, bro?"

*"Cool, good call. I wonder if dip shit has
had to use his windshield wipers yet?*

"Dude, let it go."

Chapter Six—That Little Prick

Mike the Sailor and Denise start to leave the Prom and get into Mike's Jeep, when Denise notices something unusual.

"Mike, my seat's wet."

Mike reaches in his glove compartment, pulls out such napkins and wipes down the seat. He notices that it's not water.

"That little prick."

"What?"

*"Your little buddy
peed on my seats."*

Mike wipes down his seat.

*"Amateur. I've got the
seat scotch guarded."*

"Come on, let's get out of here."

Mike starts up his Jeep, his windshield wipers go on and the shoe polish smears the entire window.

"What the?"

He's pissed.

Back at Telsa's Tavern, the guy playing against the Asian girl returns back to the table ready for another game. The Japanese girl returns and promptly freaks out.

"What you do! No, no, no. I no play you."

"Why not?"

*"You suck! Checkers easy game.
You try to get me drunk!"*

Yuien opens her purse full of bottles.

*"Look! You try take advantage of
Yuien. I no play you anymore!"*

"I'll play you."

"You play checkers."

Z nods.

"You play well?"

Z nods.

"Okay, I play you!"

*"Fine, you're just a tease, always.
Bro, I'll sell you my booze."*

"Done."

Zeus opens up his wallet to take the money out. Yuien notices exactly how much money he has in it. Guy takes the money and leaves. We see a montage of games being played. They play four games. Some z wins, some Yuien wins, they never drink their bottles, just collect them on the side. They play their final game.

"You are sooo good!"

Said in a high pitch.

"All the girls say that about me!"

Both laugh.

*"You play me again! This
time we drink! Okay?"*

"Sure."

The final pieces being moved, bottles being drunk. A crowd gathers to watch the game. When a piece is jumped, the crowd chants, *"Drink, drink, drink."* We see the game come to an end. Empty bottles are on each side of the board, there are two pieces left on the board. Z finally loses to Yuien. The crowd bursts into applause and yelling. Yuien takes the last bottle and drinks the last of the Tequila.

"You good player!"

"No no no, you're a good player!"

Crowd disburses.

"No no no, you are good player."

"No no no no, I'm not good, you're good!"

Both laugh together.

"You're funny!"

"You're cute!"

"You looking to pick up, girl?"

"Depends? Is she as cute as you?"

Yuien laughs.

*"Say, who came up with this idea of
playing chess with jack and tequila?"*

"Ernie Kovacs."

"Who is that?"

Smiling.

*"He was a pioneer in television,
kind of like the Telsa of Television."*

*"Oh, okay, good to know. Is
that your major, Communications?"*

*"Yeah, sure. I'm into making films,
if you know what I mean."*

Puffs out her chest, then presses her lips together, blows
Zeus a mini kiss and then laughs. Zeus face begins to blush.

*"I'm joking, you look like
you're in high school."*

"Why do you say that?"

*"Maybe because you're wearing a tux
and possibly went to your prom tonight?"*

Zeus shakes his head no.

> *"No, I blew off my prom just*
> *to be with you and I'm 18."*

> *"Oh, you're smooth. What's your name?"*

> *"Z."*

Yuien makes a face.

> *"Z? What's your real name?"*

> *"Zeus!"*

Yuien's eyes go wide open.

> *"You Greek?*

> *"One hundred percent!*
> *What's your name?"*

> *"Yuien, I'm Japanese."*

Zeus acts shocked and becomes a mini standup comedian.

> *"No, Japanese. I could 'a swore*
> *you were from Brooklyn."*

Zeus stands up. Yuien checks out his feet and checks out his hands.

> *"Stand up. Let me look at you.*
> *You've got big hands and feet.*
> *What your shoe size?"*

"Thirteen."

Yuien ponders the moment, then makes her decision.

*"We go back to my place. You drive it
home? I mean, you drive me home."*

"Oui, madam."

Yuien puts her hand up.

"I hate French! Don't speak French, okay?"

"From here on out, it's all Greek to me.

*Ótan ftásoume sti thési sas, tha parkáro to pink
Cadillac káto apó to olisthiró drómo.*

Translated, it means, when we get to your place, I'm going to
park the pink Cadillac down the slippery driveway. Zeus smiles.

*"I don't know what that means,
but i think i might like it."*

Yuien leads Zeus to the parking lot outside. They are hand in
hand. We see a camper.

"What's this?"

"It's my ride. You can drive?"

Zeus has an undaunted look.

"Sure."

Heinz whistles.

"Hey, where are you going?"

"I'm gonna test drive this camper."

"I can't believe you're leaving me here."

Sarcastic tone.

*"You're a big boy. You'll
find yourself a ride home."*

"Z, let's go!"

"What about your dad's car?"

"I'll pick it up later."

Yuien walks over and whispers to Zeus.

"Me so horny Z, me love you long time."

They step into Yuien's camper, shut the door and head out. Yuien is in the passenger seat and Zeus is in the driver's seat. Suddenly Yuien is all over Zeus, kissing him, rubbing him, licking him. Finally, she tells him to pull over.

*"I want you, Zeus, pull the camper over
at the next rest stop and I'll put my
diaphragm in."*

Zeus takes the exit, parks at a rest stop. Yuien starts to leave to go to the bathroom.

"Don't go away. I'll be right back."

Yuien leans over to him and gives him a kiss and proceeds to the bathroom. Zeus has an internal narration going on. *"Holy shit. I'm in jersey, driving a frickin camper. Hey, I'm in a camper. I gonna get laid! I'm gonna get laid!"* Yuien returns from the restroom. Yuien takes Zeus's hand, and they leave the cab, pulling the shades as to have privacy.

Yuien and Zeus are making out. Yuien removes her top, leaving her brassiere on. She and Zeus start taking the rest of each other's clothes off. Yuien and Zeus are heavily making out. Zeus takes off his shorts, Yuien's eyes get big. Zeus is just too big to get in without a little help.

"Ooh, i want you inside me."

"That's good, cause I want to be inside."

*"Go to the bathroom and get the tube in
medicine cabinet. That should do the trick."*

"Okay."

Zeus gets up and makes a beeline for the bathroom while trying to hurry and look cool. He searches and searches but can only find some toothpaste and something his parents have that he thought was for hemorrhoids.

*"Are you sure it's in here? Cause, all I can
find is toothpaste and hemorrhoid medicine."*

Yuien lying in completely confused.

"Hemorrhoid medicine?"

"Yeah, this k y stuff."

She laughs.

*"KY's not for hemorrhoids, k y's
is lubrication for easier penetration."*

Zeus walks out of the bathroom with the KY.

"No way."

"No, really."

"My parents have this stuff."

Zeus is obvious grossed out by the thought of his parents having sex. He's lost that love feeling. Yuien takes the KY from Zeus, looks down at his manhood.

"That's not going to do."

Yuien puts some KY on her hand. Proceeds to cozy up to Zeus, whispering stuff in his ear. Zeus is still apprehensive.

"I don't know about this?"

Yuien starts stroking Zeus. His eyes roll into the back of his head.

"You like now?"

Zeus doesn't respond. He continues his own internal commentary of himself, finally getting laid. *"F the Prom, I'm getting my dick stroked. This rule, I'm going to get laid."* We hear a knock at the door of the camper. It startles Yuien.

"What's that?"

"What's what?"

Yuien stops. We see red lights flashing leaking through the curtains.

"Don't stop!"

There's another knock on the camper door. Zeus looks at Yuien.

"It's the Po Po?"

"Oh shit, what do they want?"

"What are you looking at me for? Answer the door?"

Zeus puts on his trousers, opens the door, and sees an Undercover Cop with his badge out.

"Can I help you, Officer?

"Sir, are you aware you are with a prostitute?"

Zeus
Prostitute? She a college student?

"Sir, I am going to have to ask
you to get out of the vehicle."

"Why?"

"Sir, please step out of the vehicle."

Zeus just in his pants gets out of the camper.

*"Sir, could you please stand by
my car. And I am going to need
to see some identification."*

Yuien starts yelling at the police officer in Japanese. She topless cover her chest with one of her arms.

*"Sorosoro oo shiri wo koko ni motsu te iku jikan desu. kodomo
wa no you ni burasagat te iru ma kare no zaifu wo te ni ire
、 okane wo tori sorekara de masho yo koko wa."*

The translation is the equivalent to *"It's about time you got ass here. The kid's hung like a horse. Get his wallet, take the money and let's get out of here."* The man, Jeremy, responds in Japanese, which puzzles Zeus. Yuien and the Jeremy carry on the conversation in Japanese.

*"Negi wo totto te i ta watashi
ni kyukei wo atae te kudasai."*

Give me a break, I was taking a leek.

*"Negi no watashi no oo shiri wo torik te 、
anata wa osoraku watashi tachi wo mi te i ta mado
koshi ni tataki nomeshi te 、 butsukari au. freek da."*

Which means, *"I was taking a leek my ass. You were probably watching us through the window and whacking off. Freak."*

*"Freek! watashi wa freek desu ka? Anata
wa ikutsu ka no kokou wo nade te iru
kodomo no pole to watashi wa freek desu ka?"*

Translation: *"Freak! I'm the freak? You're stroking some high school kid's pole and I'm the freak?"*

"Tada okane wo te ni ire te ,
koko kara de masho yo."

Translation: *"Just get the money and let's get out of here."*

Jeremy and Yuien return to speaking English to clue Zeus into knowing what's going on.

"Maam, you're going to need to get dressed,
because I'm arresting you and your friend for
prostitution and solicitation of prostitution."

"Bite me Five-O!"

Yuien slams the camper door shut. Faked Cop, Jeremy turns his attention back to Zeus. He walks towards to his car.

"Put your wallet on the hood, turn
around spread your legs apart
and place your hands on the hood."

Zeus obliges, allowing Jermey to position himself to go through Zeus's wallet.

"I don't understand Officer."

The Conman is now taking Zeus's money from his wallet. He looks at Zeus's ID.

"Well, here's the situation.
Your underage, intoxicated and in a
vehicle with a known prostitute."

"She told me she was a college student."

"Why should I believe you?"

*"Look, my date dumped me at
the Prom, I got thrown out for
fighting the guy. So then my
buddy and I go to this bar."*

"Stop, I don't want to hear another word."

Jeremy hands Zeus back his wallet, minus his money.

*"Here's your wallet. I want you to go get your Tux
on and get out of here. I never saw you, you never
saw me. You keep your mouth shut and go back to
Pennsylvania or I run your ass in, and you will be
charged with Public Intoxication, DUI, Solicitation
of Prostitution and Possession of a Stolen Vehicle."*

The door to the camper opens Yuien comes out. The Mock
Officer pulls out his handcuffs and speaks to.

"Maam, put your hands behind your head."

Yuien does as the officer instructs. It now appears as if she's
done this a time or two.

"Kinky cop, that will cost you extra."

"Hands above your head, please."

He puts the cuffs on her.

"What's the charge time?"

"Public drunkenness."

"That's a laugh."

*"We'll see how funny you think it is when you
have to bail yourself out. You're lucky, it's only
a misdemeanor, I could charge with solicitation
of Prostitution. So stop your crying, I'm letting
your "Little Buddy go with a warning."*

He puts Yuien in the back of his car and leaves the scene with Yuien. Zeus goes back into the camper, gets dresses, then goes to a pay phone and dials.

Zeus's mother is ironing. The phone rings, she answers it. There is a brief conversation, mainly yes's, okay's and I be right there. Ma picks up the phone and calls a neighbor.

*"Hello, Mrs. Janikowski? Yes, how are you? I've got to
go out for a couple of hours. Do you think you could
watch Adonis? Great, thank you. I'll bring him right over."*

As Zeus's mom leaves, we see Zeus at a rest stop snack area. He is hungry and decides to get a candy bar from a vending machine. He reaches into his back pocket and gets his wallet. To his surprise, all of his money is gone. He looks confused and starts looking over every inch of his wallet for his money. It suddenly dons on him that
she's been had.

"No way! Can this night get any worse?"

Chapter Seven—There Was An Accident

Zeus finally makes it home. Zeus enters his house, and the Grandfather Clock is striking 3 am. We hear a second set of footsteps. Zeus is trying to walk through the house quietly, as not to wake anyone up. Zeus's brother, Adonis, is fast asleep in Socrates' chair, which strikes Zeus as odd, but he proceeds to the kitchen, where a light is on. Zeus assumes it's his mother who is up and was worried about him. Zeus opens the kitchen door.

"Ma, you didn't have to stay up."

Zeus immediately stops talking when he sees that it's his dad and not his mom.

"Pops, what are you doing up?"

Socrates is somber.

*"I need to talk with you about
something very serious."*

Zeus goes into damage control mode as to the evening's activities.

*"I know Pops and I apologize. I
swear it'll never happen again."*

"What are you talking about?"

Zeus quickly changes the subject, thinking he might not be busted.

"I don't know. What are you talking about?"

"There was an accident tonight."

"Oh, no."

Runs to the kitchen window to see his Pinto.

"Pop, where's the Pinto?"

Socrates now starts to breakdown.

"Your mother, she loved you very much."

Zeus is freaked out because his dad is crying. Zeus has never seen his dad cry.

"Where's ma? Is she okay? Where's ma?"

"Your mother she…"

Zeus goes running towards his parents' bedroom yelling for his mother.

"Mom, mom."

Socrates has gotten up and is now in the hallway, as Zeus makes his way back to the kitchen.

*"Zeus, please be quiet. You'll wake your
brother. Come with me to the kitchen."*

They walk back to the kitchen. Sensing what has gone on, those second set of footsteps, Heinz, puts Socrates' car keys on the hook in the family room and silently leaves.

Days later at Cemetery, we are at a small, maybe 15 to 20 people are at Zeus's mother's funeral. We hear the last words of the preacher.

*"We commit her body to the ground, earth to earth,
Ashes to ashes, Dust to dust; in complete assurance
and undeniable faith of her resurrection unto
eternal life. Amen."*

A moment of silence, then everyone pays Socrates their respects. He lets everyone know that there will be a celebration of life and the Diner.

People are mingling around the diner. We see Zeus talking with his father. Suddenly we see a gentleman is his mid 30's walks up to Socrates and Zeus. It's the black sheep of the family, Socrates' youngest brother, Dimitri. Socrates is not happy with his brother's appearance.

"I'm so sorry about your mother."

"I told you, don't come around there. Leave."

*"Look, we're family and I'm here to help
you out, however you need me too."*

*"You're going to help me? What?
Taking my money? Leave, leave now!"*

Dimitri smiles, shakes Zeus's hand, and leaves out a side door, before anyone really notices. Zeus follows him out of the restaurant.

*"Uncle Dimitri don't leave. Pops,
just isn't thinking straight."*

Dimitri starts to get into his convertible.

"Whoa, so this is what you roll in?"

"Yeah."

"Sweet! I wish I had a car like that."

Socrates has walked out of the restaurant to have a smoke.

"All it takes is a little hard work and..."

Zeus interrupts.

"I know a college diploma."

"The old man is on your back about college, huh?"

"Yeah, he's pretty hardcore about it."

"Yeah, he tried that with me too."

Socrates steps out into plain sight. He flicks the butt of the cigarette he just smoked.

"You think I like to crack the whip?"

"Pop, how long have you been out here?"

"Long enough. You don't want to go to college?"

"I don't know Pop. I honestly don't know."

Socrates looks at Dimitri and begins to speak.

"You really want to help?"

*"Yeah, of course i do, that's why I'm
here, we're family, and we're blood."*

"Okay, then you do this for me. You take Zeus with you. You let him work for you this summer. Okay?"

"Yeah, no problem. I could use the help."

Pop, I can't go. Who'll watch Adonis?

"Your brother is not your concern. You go with your uncle and you decide if you want to go to college or you work.

"But?"

"No buts, no excuses, no meddling father. You, Zeus, you decided. You choose, I pay for your college, or I give the money your mother and I saved for you to go to college. You think about it and then you come home after the Summer, you tell me your decision. Deal?

Zeus is stunned. Socrates has made him an offer he can't refuse. Zeus is in a state of shock.

"Deal?"

Zeus looks at Dimitri for his approval.

"Uncle Dimitri?"

"Yeah, I told your dad, anything I could do to help."

"Okay pop, deal."

"Ah, one more thing, you take the dog with you."

Extends his hand towards his father's hand. Socrates pulls Zeus in for a hug and whispers into his ear.

"I love you son."

Socrates then releases Zeus. Zeus is now all choked up and about to get emotional.

*"Dimitri, take the boy before he changes
his mind and I have two troublemakers
to deal with."*

*"Wow, okay, this shit is happening so quick,
let me say, "goodbye to Adonis and Heinz".*

Zeus goes back into the restaurant to say goodbye to Adonis and Heinz. Socrates extends hand to Dimitri, they shake, and then Socrates pulls Dimitri close to him and whispers.

"You take care of my boy."

Socrates releases Dimitri. Zeus, Heinz, and Adonis come out of the restaurant. Adonis doesn't really know Dimitri.

"Uncle Dimitri, this is my best friend, Heinz.

How you doing, kid?

*"Good. I sounds like you're
taking my boy as slave labor."*

"Yeah, I get him at the relative's discount."

*"I hear ya. Z, it's not gonna be
Summer around her without you."*

*"Hey, I'll take some more slave
labor, if you're offering?"*

"I wish I could, but I've already got a job."

*"Are you sure? Cause the girls of
the Outer Banks are extremely hot!"*

Zeus smiles.

*"Maybe I can come for a weekend
and partake in the babe-o-rama."*

"Bro, that sounds totally babelicious."

*"Hey Adonis, is it okay if I steal your
brother to help me out at my diner
for a while."*

"Yeah, but make sure you bring him back."

"Deal, done."

Adonis and Dimitri shake hands.

*"Come on Z, let's hit it. We'll stop by the
house get some of your stuff and head
back to the Outer Banks".*

Zeus and Heinz punch fists. Zeus leaves with Dimitri.

Zeus's home, Zeus is in his room, finishing packing a duffel bag with his clothes. He finishes packing and heads down to the kitchen. He sets the duffel bag down on the counter and goes to the fridge for a drink.

Pulls out the drink, goes to the cupboard, gets a class, pours the drink and is reflective of his times in the kitchen with mother. Sudden he sees a vision of his mother preparing lunch, he is shocked.

"Ma?"

His mother turns around and smiles.

"Ma, I don't get it."

She starts to speak but fades away as there is a knock on the backdoor.

*"Hello? Come on, let's hit it, we've
got a long drive ahead of us."*

Zeus looks around the kitchen. His mother is nowhere in sight. He washes the glass, puts it in the dishwasher and leaves out the backdoor. The backdoor suddenly opens, Zeus looks around to make sure his mother's really not there, notices that the kitchen light is still on, smiles, turns it off, closes the door and leaves.

Zeus, Dimitri and Zeus's Chihuahua Bingo leave Stroudsburg. Zeus is taking a visual postcard of their journey from Stroudsburg to the Outer Banks. Finally, they are arrival at Dimitri's home. Zeus grabs his bags and the three head into the house.

They drop them in the living room. Dimitri lays down the house rules.

*"Okay, here's the deal. You're eighteen, so
I'm going to treat you like a man."*

Throws Zeus a set of keys.

"These are the keys to the diner and the house."

"Thanks, so do i get a set of key for your ride?"

"Dream on, I'm going to be out of town, so you can hoof it. You stay out of my shit, I stay out of your shit. Understand?

"Yeah."

"As far as work goes, I expect you to work a full forty. What you get paid is all yours, but you pay for your own shit. Sound fair?"

"Yeah, sounds fair."

Olympia Diner, mid-morning. Dimitri and Zeus arrive at the diner. The diner is relatively busy. Dimitri is making introductions with the staff on duty.

"Zeus, this is Chanell. She's are hostess slash cashier."

"Pleasure to meet you, Zeus."

"Please, call me Z."

"Okay, nice to meet you z. Sorry to hear about your mother."

"Thanks."

"Well, if you ever need a woman's prospective."

Angelo enters on the scene and takes exception to Chanell's comments.

*"What the hell would he need
a women's perspective for?*

"And this would be Angelo."

"Kid, you crotchet?"

"No."

"Have you ever had a period?"

Zeus is puzzled by Angelo's line of questioning.

"Only at the end of a sentence."

"Cute, have you ever menstruated?"

"Ah no!"

*"You're in the shower, you gotta pee,
you get out of shower or stay in?"*

"Stay in."

"I rest my case."

Dimitri interjects.

*"You have any questions, you
see either Angelo or Chanell."*

They proceed through the diner and, to Zeus's delight, there are two younger waitresses on duty. Their names are Cindy and Molly. They're both in their early twenties. Zeus is sizing them both up. Cindy definitely catches Zeus's eye.

"Cindy, Molly! Let me introduce to my nephew
Zeus, he's going to be working with us this summer.

Cindy shows no real interest in Zeus. Molly, on the other hand, is very interested in the new guy. Molly speaks up.

"Zeus, huh?"

"Yeah."

"What are you named after some
sort of Greek god or something?"

"Yeah."

"I'm named after Molly McButter, mother loved
that stuff when she was pregnant with me."

Zeus narration: Okay then. Zeus politely smiles and shakes his head. Dimitri and Zeus go to Dimitri's office. Angelo walks into the office.

"Are you done with him?"

"Yeah, he's all yours. Zeus, meet your boss."

"Oh, I thought i was going to start on Monday."

Angelo looks at Dimitri. Then back at Zeus.

*"Start Monday? We've got a full weekend
of locals and tourists to take care of."*

Dimitri looks at Zeus.

*"Yeah, okay, that's cool. I was just expecting
to have a couple of days off to get my head
together and check out the scene before I
started working."*

*"Get your head together? What is this fuckin
surgery? You're a bus boy, you clean off tables
and occasionally wash dishes."*

"Okay, I'll change and be right back."

*"No, I got a better idea. You come
back on Monday with a better attitude."*

Zeus looks at Dimitri. Dimitri shrugs his shoulders and
raises his hands.

"You heard the man."

Zeus leaves the office bewildered and feeling betrayed.

"Do you think that was really necessary?"

"Kids got to know I'm the alpha male."

*"It's a wonder you just didn't
mount him here in the office."*

"I thought about."

Olympia diner, Zeus walking through the kitchen to leave.
He meets Dimitri's other cook, Charlie. Charlie is Jamaican, he
has dreadlock and a strong accent.

*"Don't worry about Angelo, the bite is
much worse than the bark."*

"Definitely needs the decaf."

"He's a good man though."

"I'll take your word for it."

"I'm Charlie."

"I'm Zeus."

"Good to meet you."

"You too."

Zeus leaves the diner.

Chapter 8—Brown Noser

Olympia diner, Monday morning, Zeus waiting in front of the diner morning. He beats Angelo to work. Angelo is impressed, but still gives Zeus a bad time. Angelo is armed with his camcorder.

"Kind of early, aren't you kid?"

"No, not really."

*"So you're telling me you show up at
your old man's restaurant early too."*

Zeus shakes his head no.

"I didn't think so."

*"Hey, I know we got off on the wrong foot,
so just I'd show up a little early to score
some points.*

"Brown noser, huh?"

"No! I just want to be treated like everyone else.

Angelo unlocks the door, the two enter the diner. Angelo goes directly to the kitchen, Zeus starts getting the tables ready, blinds up, etc. The diner is ready for business about 15 minutes ahead of schedule. Zeus is trying to make small talk with Angelo.

"So what's the camcorder for?"

"Who are Mike Wallace?"

"No, just making conversation."

"Why?"

*"Look, I know I didn't make such
a great first impression."*

"First impressions are overrated."

"You think?"

*"Yeah, cause people always try to be
gracious and kiss your ass when you first
meet them. It's only after you've known a
person awhile, that you see the real deal."*

Zeus ponders Angelo's rap.

"Yeah, i guess you're right."

*Angelo
Falocapoochia.*

Suddenly, the front door of the diner opens. It's Chanell.
Angelo retreats to the kitchen.

"Good morning. Get you some coffee."

"Morning, sure. Give me the good stuff."

Chanell smiles. Molly comes strolling in. Looks at the clock.

"Seconds to spare Angelo!"

"Ooh, that makes three shifts in a row."

Molly flips Angelo the bird. Zeus laughs.

*"What are you laughing, kid? You don't
know where those fingers have been?"*

Molly looks at Chanell.

"How does he do that?"

"He's psycho."

Zeus joins in Molly and Chanell's conversation.

"Don't you mean psychic?"

Chanell and Molly shake their heads, "No", then respond
unison.

"No, he's psycho!"

A gambling house day, Dimitri has found a new place to
gamble called Johnny Lombardi's. He knocks on the door. A
slide window is opened on the door. This face is in the window.

"Yeah, what do you want?"

*"I heard if I want to play with the
Yankees, this is the place."*

"Oh yeah, 16 or 8 slices?"

"16 is too many to eat?"

"Mantle, Mays or Snider."

"DiMaggio!"

"Alright."

Doors opens and Dimitri enters the card game.

Meanwhile, at the Olympia diner the diner is swamped, Cindy arrives for her shift. Molly starts talking to Cindy about Zeus.

"So what's the 411?"

"Nadia Comaneci."

"How's what's his face working out?"

"You mean Zeus? He's great."

"Oh no, you've fallen for another busboy."

Molly
What he's cute?

They both are looking at Zeus clean a table. He is bent over a table and cleaning it. They are checking out his ass.

"Okay, so he's got a nice ass."

Cindy and Molly visualize Zeus in slow motion as he turns around with dish tray in hand. He smiles and winks at the girls. They both smile. Angelo walks up behind both girls and speaks.

"Why don't you two take a picture? It'll last longer."

"Sorry Angelo."

Molly goes back to work. Cindy is just standing there, in thought.

"Hello, earth to Cindy."

"Oh, hi Angelo."

*"Are you just visiting or are you
actually going to work today?"*

"Work."

"Then let's go, chop, chop."

Olympia diner, later that afternoon. Cindy is hatching a scheme to get Chanell's position in the diner. She thinks if she can get close to Zeus, then he could influence his uncle into putting Cindy in Chanell's position. Cindy's half shift is over, she asks Zeus out.

"So z, what you doing tonight?"

"Uh? Nothing, why?"

*"Well, I thought you might want some
company. I can show you around."*

Zeus is shocked by these turn of events, but extremely excited.

"Uh, sure, but I don't have any wheels."

"Don't worry, I've got a VW Bug."

"Coolio!"

*"I'll pick you up at Dimitri's,
say, at about eight?"*

"Yeah."

"Later."

"Late."

Zeus goes to the kitchen. Molly has overheard the conversation and is pissed off at Cindy.

"What the hell's your problem?"

"What?"

*"Don't give me that what bullshit,
you know what I'm talking about."*

"What, that I told Zeus I show him around town?"

The conversation is getting more intense.

"What's up with that? I told you I liked him."

Cindy
*Yeah, and you probably like ice cream too,
but it ain't going to stop me from eating it.*

"You're such a bitch."

Cindy
Excuse me?

Chanell makes her way to the girls. Who are now face to face and are about to throw down.

"What's going on?

"Nothing."

"Cindy?"

*"She butt hurt because I offered
to show Zeus around the town."*

"Bitch!"

"Watch your mouth. You're at work."

Angelo now comes out from the kitchen.

"We got a problem."

"The girls are in a dispute."

"You girls know how we handle disputes."

"I'm ready to go."

"Cindy?"

"Pfft, bring it."

A chant comes from the diner patrons, *"Fight, fight, fight."* Zeus comes out from the kitchen.

"What's going on?"

"Cindy and Molly are going to fight."

"Why?"

*"Who knows? They've got a dispute. They can't talk it out,
we take it to the back and let them duke it out."*

"You're kidding right?"

*"Nope, do me a favor, go flip the open
sign to closed and lock the front door."*

"Okay?"

"Everybody to the back of diner."

We follow everyone to behind the diner. We see Angelo, Cindy and Molly. Angelo is giving them instructions.

*"Alright, I want a fair fight, no hair pulling,
no below the belt and know that after the fight is
over, so is the dispute. You girls have anything
to each other?"*

"I'm going to knock your block off."

We then see that the girls aren't going to actually fight, but instead play the iconic game of Rockem Sockem Robots. Cindy just smiles and motions her hand to "Bring it". The girls are now face to face in a boxing stare down.

"Let's get it on!"

The girls are sitting at a makeshift table and our fighting with Rock'em Sock'em robots. It's a grueling fight, but eventually Cindy knocks Molly's block off. Cindy is smug. Molly begrudgingly shakes Cindy's hand. The crowd disburses, some back to the diner, some just leave.

A gambling house, evening Dimitri has a cigar in his mouth. He's been on a winning streak and is about to cash out.

*"I don't think I've ever had a
run like that? I was on fire."*

"Stick around. I'll take care of that."

*"I think I'll pass for now. I'm going to get
a good steak, some good scotch and get laid.
See you boys around."*

"You'll be back."

We then see a montage of Cindy flirting with Zeus at the diner. Zeus and Cindy on dates, walking on the beach holding hands at sunset, kissing on the beach, finally in bed. Zeus has finally scored, had sex and it seems to have blossomed him into being more outgoing.

Dimitri's house, afternoon. Heinz drives up to Dimitri's house and calls Zeus on his cell phone to Dimitri's landline. He disguises his voice as a feminine man.

"Yes, hello, I'm calling for the Greek god of love, Zeus."

Zeus is in the kitchen.

"Who is this?"

Heinz continuing his charade.

*"That's not important right now. What's
important is that you are he, that he is you."*

Zeus is in the kitchen.

*"Look, I don't know what you're talking
about. Who you are anyway and how'd
you got this number?"*

Heinz continuing his charade.

*"Oh, okay, well you don't know me, but
my name is Sidney Lipschitz. I got name
out of the g & l 's swingers hookup."*

Zeus is puzzled.

"You got my name? Where?"

*"You know the ad you placed in the gay & lesbian
swingers hookup? It's right here in the July's classified
ads. Here I'll ready you your ad. "young, hung and
looking for fun in all the wrong places."*

Heinz starting to crack up. Zeus starting to get mad.

*"Look, I'm straight okay. Obviously, somebody
was trying to play a joke. Not a funny one,
but a joke."*

Heinz continuing his charade.

"Who would do such a thing? What a vlaka."

Zeus realizes that it's Heinz.

*"Asshole! Funny, real funny. What it be?
So when are you going to come and visit me?"*

Heinz knocks on Dimitri's door.

"Hold on, somebody's knocking on the front door.

Zeus hears the knock on Dimitri's door. Zeus is walking to
the front door while he's talking to Heinz.

*"Bro, that's weird, somebody's
knocking on my door, too."*

Zeus opens the front door, and it's Heinz.

"What the… you sneaky bastard."

Zeus opens the screen door. The two hug and then come back into Dimitri's house. They sit down at the kitchen table and start catching up.

"So, it's looks like you enjoy the bachelor's life?"

"Bro, not living with your parents' rules!"

*"No shit, dumbass, that's exactly
why you should go to college?"*

A nude Cindy walks out of the bedroom.

*"Why go to college when you can wake
up with this every morning?"*

"Oh shit!"

Zeus is shocked, he gets up from the kitchen table and hustles Cindy back into the bedroom.

"What the hell did you do that for?"

*"I'm so sick of this college bullshit. What's wrong
With just working hard and having a good time?"*

*"Look, I really don't want to open up that can
right now, Heinz is here, you're here, life is good.
Why don't you get dressed and we'll go out to dinner?"*

*"I've got a better idea. Why don't you tell your friend to
watch some tv and we'll take a shower and clean some of
up some of those dirty thoughts you're having."*

"Okay?"

Zeus opens the door.

*"Hey, we're going to take a shower
and then we'll go out to dinner, okay?"*

"Alright, I'll just make myself at home."

Zeus closes the door. We see Heinz getting a glass from the
cupboard. Heinz has the glass pressed up against the wall and is
trying to listen to what is going on behind closed doors.
Suddenly the bedroom door opens. Heinz nervously drops the
glass which falls behind the couch.

"You ready?"

"Ah, yeah."

Cindy comes out of the bedroom.

"Cindy, this is my best friend, Heinz."

Cindy put off by Heinz's college talk and presence.

*"Sorry about you having to see
my delta gammas, frat boy!"*

"No problem, always willing to take one for the team."

*"Yeah, Zeus doesn't seem to have
a problem with them either.*

"Okay? Let's go to the diner for some dinner."

Cindy smiles at Zeus, then takes his hand and the three leave Dimitri's.

"Okay."

Olympia diner, later Cindy, Heinz, and Zeus are finishing their meals at the dinner. Chanell comes to see what's up.

"Hey, what are you kids up to?"

*"Just grabbing some grub before we
show my friend Heinz the nightlife."*

"Nice to meet you Heinz."

"No, the pleasure is all mine, Mrs. Robinson."

"Dude, you can't be hitting on one of my bosses."

Chanell smiles and laughs.

*"Bro, it's all copasetic. I'm only here for
the night. If we were to bounce the bed
springs, no harm, no foul, right Mrs. R?"*

"Exactly, you into S & M?"

"Sure, S & M, M & M 's all that stuff. I like it all.

*"Really? Cause I just love disciplining naughty boys.
I like getting my strap on and punishing them.*

A look comes over Heinz's face like this is cool. Zeus doesn't know what to make out of the conversation and Cindy she just has a smirk on her face. Heinz thinks he's going to get laid.

"Ah, yeah, that sounds cool,
when do you get off?"

"Eleven thirty."

"Well, then I just a roll on over."

"Okay."

Chanell is being called to the front of the diner. Heinz winks at her.

"I gotta go. I'll see you at eleven thirty."

"Until then, my love."

Chanell leaves. Zeus questions Heinz about know what he's doing.

"Dude, what are you doing?"

"What? I guy's got experience life, don't he?"

Cindy chimes into the conversation.

"You're going to let her put a
strap on a dildo, and do you?"

"What?"

Cindy cannot believe Heinz's naivety.

*"You don't know what you
got yourself into, do you?"*

It dons on Zeus what Chanell had been talking about.

*"Wait a minute. Did you just say,
a strap on a dildo and do him?"*

*"Yeah, you Pennsylvanian boys
don't get out much, do you?"*

"I guess not."

*"Yo, what is your girl talking about?
Hip me to the 411 going on here."*

*"She's a dominatrix, which means she's
into humiliating guys, punishing them with
whips and all sorts of sick devices."*

*"What? Fuck that, Bro let's dip, I ain't going
from a tight end to a wide receiver. So,
let's break wind and get out of here."*

They all start to get up and Angelo approaches the table.

"You must be Heinz?"

"Depends on who's asking."

"Heinz, this is Angelo."

"Oh, how's it going?"

*"Pretty good, Chanell over there
tells me you're a swinger."*

*"Yeah, I pretty much let it all hang
out, if you know what I mean."*

*"I hear ya, so then tonight you
would mind a threesome?"*

"Cool. Who's the other chick?"

*"Other chick, you're funny. No, I'm
talking about me and you tag
teaming Chanell."*

Cindy is just shaking her head on how Angelo and Chanell are fucking with both Heinz and Zeus. Heinz senses this maybe his opportunity to get out of tonight. Zeus is just in shock.

*"No, I'm not really into that whole
tag-teaming with another guy thing."*

*"Oh, well then how's about me, Chanell, Cindy,
Zeus and yourself, we have a little orgy?"*

Cindy is going along with the rouse.

*"Yeah, I'm down with that. We haven't
had a good orgy since Dimitri left."*

A look of horror has entered both Heinz's and Zeus's faces.

"Come on z, it'll be fun?"

Zeus is speechless. Angelo speaks up.

*"What is wrong with you two?
We're just fucking with you."*

A sense of relief has come over both Heinz and Zeus.

"I knew that."

"Yeah, sure you did. Angelo rule #85, be careful of what you wish for. So how was your dinner, Heinz.

"Dude, it was the shit!"

"Say Again."

"It was the shit!"

Angelo looks at Zeus.

Yeah, it annihilated.

Now the boys are fucking with Angelo. Angelo looks at Cindy.

"It was good. They both enjoyed it."

Angelo shakes his head and leaves. Angelo walks up to Chanell.

"You know my cooking is the shit?"

"What?"

"My cooking it's the shit?"

"Oh yeah, but does it annihilate?"

"Yeah."

"That's sick."

"What? Sick, no, it means people it like."

"Yeah, I know, sick means cool."

"Falocapoochia."

Cindy, Heinz, and Zeus having fun at Turner's Raw Bar in the town of Avon, North Carolina.

"This club beat Hula Hoops all to hell, this place is off the hook."

"Yeah, it's hella tight."

"Yeah, unless you've lived here all your life."

"Nice place to be from?"

"Exactly."

"The only thing this club doesn't have is karaoke."

"I didn't know you could sing?"

"Don't worry, he can't. You don't want to hear what comes out of his mouth."

"What are you talking about? Check this out Cin."

Zeus clears his throat and begins to butcher "The Doors," Roadhouse Blues.

"I woke up this morning And I shot myself a deer."

"I rest my case."

"What song was that?"

"Oh common, it's an American classic."

Heinz shakes his head in disbelief.

"I warned you."

*"Okay, do it again and I'll close
my eyes and concentrate."*

*"I woke up this morning, and I shot myself
a deer. Outside of the roadhouse, they got
some Buffalo's."*

Cindy opens her eyes, has a confused look on her face, and is about to crack up.

"Come, it's Jim Morrison, it's the Doors."

*"More like, lock your doors and hide
you children from your singing."*

Cindy bust out laughing. Heinz and Zeus join in laughing. They all share a good laugh. Cindy excuses herself to the restroom.

"I'll be right back."

She gives Zeus a kiss.

*"Bro, I don't think I've
ever seen you so happy?"*

"Yeah, I…"

Their conversation is rudely interrupted by three local guys, friends of Cindy's ex-boyfriend, Eddie.

"Hey you, slap happy!"

Heinz and Zeus look at each other. Certainly, they're not talking to us.

"Yeah, you dipshit."

"Are you talking to me?"

"Yeah, I'm talking to you."

"What?"

"If you know what's good for you,
you'll stop seeing Cindy."

Heinz joins the conversation.

"Who the fuck are you? Her dad."

"No, but we're the guys wo are
going to kick your asses.

Cindy comes back from the restroom.

"What's going on?"

"Cindy, how's it going? We were just getting
Acquainted with your new friends. We gotta
go, we'll catch up with you boys later."

"Look forward to it Sally."

The three locals leave. Cindy sits down.

"What did they say?"

"Nothing that made any sense."

"Pft, they told Z to stop seeing you."

"Don't worry about those guys. They're idiots. Their combined IQ wouldn't even measure up to a chimpanzee.

"So who are they?"

"They're friends of my ex-boyfriend Eddie. They follow him around like he's some sort of sports legend."

"Sports legend?"

"Yeah, Eddie was the star of the football team, yeah, he got a scholarship to FU."

"F me."

"No FU!"

"You can't say that to my best friend, FU Cindy."

"You can't say that to Cindy. FU, Heinz."

"Oh yeah, well when FU, Z."

Cindy
Fuz?

They all laugh and continue to party.

Chapter Nine—School Of Hard Knocks

Zeus is getting ready for work. Heinz is also awake; he is preparing to go back home.

*"Z, got to admit, I was worried about
you and how you were doing?"*

"Thanks bro."

"But looks like you've got it all dialed in."

*"Well, I wouldn't say I've got it all dialed,
but i am really having a great time."*

"Yeah, it shows."

*"Okay, well, I guess, I guess this
is it until the next time?"*

*"Yeah, next time you come back home and
see me. Oh yeah, I almost forgot. Denise's
boyfriend dumped her. She said to say, Hi and
that she misses you".*

"Really, that's random."

Cindy enters the room naked again.

"Tell the Bitch, I said, Hi too."

Cindy goes back into the bedroom.

"Don't ever leave that chick, she rules!"

Heinz and Zeus shake hands, punch fists.

*"Now go get a quickie
before you go to work."*

Heinz leaves Dimitri's.

Hours later, Angelo and Zeus are opening the diner.

"Hey, can I ask you a question?"

"Yeah."

"You think you're in love, don't you?"

"Yeah, Cindy's great."

*"Please tell me, you're not stupid enough
to be thinking about getting married."*

"Well actually? Yeah, I have been? She's great."

"How many women you been with?"

"Lots."

Angelo gives him a look like that's bullshit.

"Okay, well, there's been Cindy and ah."

"And... your right hand."

*"Okay, so Cindy is the only girl I ever
had sex with, but it's magical when
we're together."*

*"What does she pull a rabbit
out of her snatch."*

*"What do you know about
love Mr. Lone Wolf?"*

*"I know enough to know that I don't
let the small head make decisions for
the big head."*

*"What are saying? I'm letting my
dick do my thinking?"*

"If the foo shits, wear it."

Olympia diner kitchen. Later that afternoon, Zeus is the back with Charlie washing dishes and rapping.

*"I don't get it Charlie, everyone's always on
my case. If it's not about college, it's about
Cindy, it's always something."*

*"Listen maan, deeses people you think are
hassling you, really care about you. They
looking out for your best interests."*

"So, what are you agreeing with Angelo and Molly?"

*"I'm not agreeing with anybody man. But you
got to know dat every action has a reaction."*

Suddenly there's a disturbance in the diner. It's Cindy's ex-boyfriend Eddie, home from college with three of his friends. Charlie and Zeus look through the pass the food place of the diner to see what exactly is going on. There is a very loud conversation going on between Cindy and Eddie.

*"So what's this? I hear your banging
some guy from the diner?"*

"What?"

"Where's old lover boy? I'm gonna kick his ass."

*"Look, it's none of your business, who I see
or who I screw, you gave up that right
when you left."*

*"Yeah, I heard from Jeff that you were letting
the kid punch the time clock, so you can get
a promotion."*

*"Don't judge me, Eddie. You just left me here, while you
went off to college. Going to your frat parties, sorority girls
and to play football. What was I supposed to do? Just sit
around with a vibrator waiting for your triumph return.
So that when you come home, you've got a familiar fuck?
So yeah Eddie, I let Zeus do me and you know what? He's
fantastic, he eats pussy better than a lesbian."*

"Where is he? I'm really going to fuck him up now!"

Eddie and his friend's head towards the kitchen. Charlie and Zeus watching the guys coming back.

*"Now dat's the reaction. Get your
board and get out of here?"*

"Yeah, but there's four guys."

*"Go, diss isn't my first
rodeo I'll be fine."*

Zeus leaves out the back door with his skateboard. Charlie looks around the kitchen for something to thwart off Eddie and his friends.

He picks up a butcher's knife. Eddie and his friends come in through the swinging door and stop dead in her tracks.

"Now, where you think you're going?"

"Ah sorry, we thought this was the bathroom."

"Well, it's not, so get your ass out of my kitchen."

"Sorry about that bro."

They turnaround and leave through the swinging door. Eddie's friend Rory sees that Cindy is motioning to someone out the window.

"There he is Eddie!"

"Let's get him."

The four boys go running out of the diner and get into Eddie's car and peel off to go get Zeus. A chase scene ensues. Finally Zeus thinks he loses them. He is relieved. He turns around to head back towards the diner, when out of nowhere Eddie cold cocks Zeus from behind and starts pummeling on Zeus, who is unable to mount any offense. Eddie leaves Zeus lying bloody and beaten. Zeus is taking his time to reflect. He bows his head and starts talking to his departed mother.

"Ma, I could really use a hug."

Still collecting his thoughts from the beat down he just took, Zeus thinks he's talking to his mother.

"I bet you could."

Zeus looks up and sees his departed mother.

"Ma, I miss you so much."

"I miss you too, my handsome boy."

"Ma, my life has been so out of control. My prom date dumped me, then I got involved with this Japanese prostitute, an undercover cop shows up, they took all my money, you die, dad sent me here, Uncle Dimitri bailed on me, then I got involved with a girl that already had a boyfriend and he just beat me up."

"Zeus, follow your heart, be your own man, be your own vision."

Ma starts to vanish, and Angelo appears.

"Hey, you alright?"

Zeus shakes his head as to shake the cobwebs out.

"Yeah, there for a minute. I thought you were my mother."

"I've been mistaken for a few people in my life, but never someone's mother."

"It was like she was right here."

"Adrenaline will do that to you."

"How'd you find me?"

"Charlie called me, said you were in some deep shit and might need my help. Come on let me take you back to Dimitri's."

They start walking to Angelo's car.

"Okay, hey thanks Angelo."

"No problem kid."

Angelo's car, Angelo and Zeus are talking about life.

*"I've got so many questions, but nobody
to ask now that my mother's gone.
She was my anchor."*

"What about your old man?"

"We don't interact with each other very well."

*"I understand, me and my father
were kind of like that too."*

"Really?"

"Yeah."

"So, how did you get to be so worldly?"

"School of hard knocks."

"Did you go to college?"

"No, I wish I did."

"Why?"

*"You don't pass a class in college; you
take it again. On the streets, you don't pass,
you die.*

"I get it."

"Do you?"

Angelo and Zeus continue to talk while they're driving to Dimitri's. They eventually pull up to Dimitri's driveway, Zeus gets out.

"Thanks Angelo."

Angelo gives a two-finger salute.

"See you tomorrow."

Angelo smiles.

"Hasta Manana"

Zeus goes in the house. Angelo puts the car in reverse and leaves.

Chapter Ten—Turkey And Gravy Sandwich

Olympia diner kitchen, morning after Zeus's beat down. Angelo and Zeus in the kitchen discussing Zeus's ass kicking.

*"You just need to let it go,
chalk it up as a life lesson."*

"Yeah, but I didn't do anything wrong."

*"Zeus, life isn't always fair, life isn't
Always about right and wrong. It's
unpredictable. No day is ever the same."*

*"Easy for you to say. You didn't
just get your ass kicked."*

*"Z, believe or not, I've had my ass kicked
more times than I can even remember."*

"Really?"

"Yeah."

*"How can you be so cool with getting
your ass kicked? You got even with
them though, didn't you?"*

*"Yeah, some of them I did, but you know what?
I learned a long time ago, don't hold a grudge.
It's just baggage you carry around and for what?
Cause some guy was bigger than you? Quicker
than you?*

Zeus pondering Angelo's statement.

"Let me clue you in on something the most dangerous weapon a man's got, it's his mind. It works a million miles a minute. You don't use it, you're at the whim of others, but, if you use your mind wisely, the world is your playground and sometimes Z. Your mind can be the ultimate "Fuck You"."

Eddie and his friends are sitting in a booth and are ready to order. Molly takes their order.

"What's up guys? Ready to order?"

"Yeah, I'll take the turkey with gravy sandwich and I'll have a milk to drink."

"Square route that."

"Yeah, take it to the third."

"I guess I'll make in unanimous."

"Okay, that's four turkey with gravy sandwiches and four milks."

"Yeah."

Molly starts to take the menu's.

"Okay, thanks guys."

Molly brings Angelo the order.

"Can I get four turkey with gravy sandwiches for Eddie and his crew."

"Eddie?"

"Yeah."

Angelo and Zeus look and see Eddie and his cronies sitting in a booth, cutting up and generally acting stupid.

"So, that's the guy who fucked you up?"

Zeus is angry.

"Yeah."

*"Cool your jets. Didn't you
hear a word I just said."*

"What?"

*"What's the most dangerous
weapon you've got?"*

"My mind."

"That's right!"

"So, what do you expect me to do?"

"Are you Greeks always this thick?"

"I don't understand what you're saying."

"This is your chance to get even."

"How? I'm not following you."

*"Normally I'd never suggest something like this,
but this is a special occasion. You know how to
make a turkey with gravy sandwich, right?"*

*"Yeah, but what does it have
to do with getting even?"*

"Can your dog really do that trick?"

"Uh huh, why?"

*"Might I suggest you give that prick a real
reason to have a shit-eating grin on his face."*

"That's sick."

"You want payback? Here's your opportunity."

Zeus calls for his dog.

"Bingo!"

Minutes later, Molly brings out the order. Eddie and his pals are wolfing the food down. Just as Eddie is finishing his sandwich, Zeus appears at the booth. Eddie admires his handy work.

*"My goodness, what happened to you?
Did you have some sort of accident?"*

Zeus smile laughs and acknowledges that he deserved what he got.

*"Hey, look, I deserved to get my
ass kicked. Lunch is on me."*

Zeus extends his hand in friendship.

"What did you do? Spit on my food."

"No, come on, that's childish."

Angelo sends Bingo into the diner. Bingo comes up to Zeus as he talks with Eddie.

"Oh, bingo. Now be a good dog. Shit."

Bingo gets into the crapping position.

"I mean sit."

Bingo craps on the floor. Eddie turns white as a ghost, runs out of the diner, and starts throwing up. His friends follow. Angelo comes out of the kitchen. Everybody is looking out the window and Eddie and his pals throwing up. The whole diner laughing at Eddie and his crew. Too embarrassed to come back in, Eddie and his boys take off. Angelo has a smile on his face and approaches Zeus.

"See, I told you the mind was the ultimate, "Fuck you". You tricked him into thinking he just ate a shit sandwich. No matter how much success in life he achieves, to the people in this diner, this town, he be forever known as a shit eater."

This inspires Zeus. He cut loose Cindy and starts just hanging out with the locals and getting the total Outer Banks experience.

Olympia restaurant, morning, just before opening. We hear Z trying to convince Angelo to take the evening off.

"Ah, come on, when was the last time you left early or even took a day off? If James Brown is the hardest working man in show business, I guess that makes you the hardest working man in the diner business."

"Yeah, yeah, yeah, just be straight up
with me. What do you want?"

"You remember the brunette, with the body to die for?"

Angelo nods his head *"Yes"* in agreement.

"Well, yours truly invited her to
A romantic candle lit evening.
After hours, of course."

Angelo smiles.

"Why don't you just take
her back to Dimitri's?"

"Hello, Angelo 101. Make a woman feel like she's the most
important thing going on. If I start at the house, there is
no place to finish a beautiful evening. If she comes to the
diner, she won't feel threatened cause she's in a public place,
thus making it easier for her to give into the Z man's charms.

"The Z man? So now you're talking
about yourself in the third person."

"Come on Ang, put yourself in my shoes. You're
18, a beautiful woman wants a romantic dinner
and then to give herself to you."

Angelo pondering Zeus's rap.

"Okay, okay. I guess I was young once. Here's the drill... I
leave when the diner closes, you lock up and have your
romantic night, but you're out of here no later the eleven,
because I got to make the deposit. Deal?"

"Deal."

The two shake hands and go back to work. The day is a breeze, with the regulars and a handful tourist traffic. Zeus is really busting ass, as he wants to make the evening special. Z is pleading with Angelo to leave the diner, even though his date hasn't arrived.

"Come on, you promised, when
The diner closed you'd go."

"Yeah, but she ain't here."

"She's gonna show. It's all good."

"Alright, but if she doesn't show, give me
a call over at the Chanell's house. You can
have dinner with us."

"Wait a minute, I thought you two
couldn't stand each other?"

"Angelo rule number 15, things
aren't always as they appear."

"Well, don't do anything I wouldn't do."

"Yeah, whatever. Damn, I'm almost
forgot to water the plants."

"What?"

"Yeah, I water them every
night before I go home."

"No, you don't."

"Sure I do. You just never saw me do it."

Angelo starts watering the plants. Zeus has a running monologue as Angelo waters the plants. Suddenly, there's a knock on the door. Zeus shoos Angelo out the backdoor. Angelo makes like a ninja and disappears into the night. Zeus is doing last-minute touch-ups to the table, there's another knock on the door. Zeus goes to open the door.

Chanell's house. Angelo has a bottle of wine, and some flowers night Chanell's door opens, Angelo kind of awkwardly hands her some flowers.

"I thought maybe you'd like some flowers,
they were going to throw them out, so I
got'em for you."

"You really know how to woo a broad, don't you?

Sarcastically said. They both smile and laugh, as if it's some sort of inside joke.

"Come on in. The lasagna is almost ready."

They both enter the house.

Dimitri gambling at Johnny Lombardi's. Dimitri is losing big time.

"I know I'm down a few, but I'm good for
the money. I own a diner on the Outer Banks."

The dealer looks at a Johnny. Johnny talks to Dimitri.

"Let me see your wallet."

"My wallet?"

"Yeah, it tells a lot about a person."

"Really? Go for it."

Dimitri hands Johnny his wallet. Johnny opens Dimitri's wallet.

"That's good."

"What?"

*"Four major credit cards,
auto club, let's see the bills."*

"Look at the bills? For what?"

*"To see if they're sequential or
are they just tossed in there?"*

"What difference does that make?"

*"If they're sequential, it tends to mean
you're orderly and have your shit together."*

"What if you don't have your bills sequential?"

*"Well, this is generalizing, but it usually
means you don't have your shit together."*

"So this is what you base you're credit lines on?"

*"No, it's a combination of things, the
bills, credit cards, photos, condoms."*

"Condoms?"

*"Yeah, you know they've got expiration
dates on them, right?"*

"Yeah, so?"

*"A man rolls around with expired condoms,
he's living dangerously. I don't extend a line
to them, but I'll give'em credit for at least
carrying the rubber."*

Looks at the bills.

"Sequential."

"So I get the line?"

"Not so fast. I gotta take a look at the photos."

Johnny starts looking, when all of a sudden, he gets this
weird look on his face.

"What?"

"Who's the guy with you in the fatigues?"

"A buddy of mine from the service."

"You keep in touch with this guy?"

"Yeah, he runs my diner."

*"Really? Where'd you
say your diner was?"*

"The Outer Banks, it's called Olympic Diner."

"Are we going to play cards or what?"

"Shut up!"

A card player starts to nervously tapping his finger on the card table. Dimitri notices he's got a couple of fingers missing. Johnny is pondering Dimitri's loan request. Dimitri asks the guy how he lost his fingers.

"What happened to your fingers?"

"Tabletop saw accident."

Johnny looks at the dealer and speaks.

"How much is he down?"

"Five."

Johnny explains the terms of the loan.

*"You win, good for you. You lose, you've
got 48 hours to pay. You don't pay on time,
you lose a finger for every hour your late.
You got past ten hours, well let's just say,
"don't be late". Capeesh?"*

"Yeah."

"You accept these terms?"

Dimitri looks at the card player, pause to really think about it and then gives the affirmative.

"Yeah."

"Spot him another five."

Chapter Eleven – I Hate Burnt Lasagna

The inside of the Chanell's house. She's giving Angelo the tour of the house.

"This is my room."

Angelo gives it the once over.

"That's funny?"

"What?"

"You don't have a collection of anything on your lying bed."

"What do you mean?"

"Well, I always pictured you as having some type of collection. I don't know, dolls, vibrators, something."

Their eyes lock, Chanell rolls her neck.

"So, do you think about me and my vibrator collection often?"

Angelo grabs her by her hips.

"Nah, just all the time."

They are just about to kiss when the timer goes off.

"You'd better get that."

"Are you sure?"

"Yeah, I hate burnt lasagna."

"Me too."

They both head towards the kitchen, postponing that kiss.

Dimitri's house, nighttime. Dimitri has been away for a couple of weeks on a gambling and partying binge. His appearance is worn out and appears disheveled. He is looking for something. His pace goes from calm to frantic in the space of about thirty seconds. He is mumbling to himself as he tears his house upside down, looking for something. After tearing the house apart to no apparent success, he sits down on his couch. Picks up the phone and calls the diner, no answer. He hangs up the phone, shakes his head angrily, gets up and leaves.

Olympia restaurant, we hear moaning going on at the diner. Sounds like Zeus's night is going well, but is it really or is there something else going on?

Chanell house, Angelo and Chanell just sitting at the table talking after their meal.

"You've got to have
some Italian in you."

"I thought you never
ask I'd love too."

She smiles.

"We'll have dessert in the bedroom."

They both get up; they go to the refrigerator, get a bottle of whip cream and head down the hallway.

Angelo's apartment complex. Dimitri is pounding on Angelo's door, yelling at the top of his lungs.

"Angelo, Angelo, Angelo!"

Dimitri continues to pound on the door, but there is no answer. Dimitri is becoming more and more frustrated. He has woken up several of Angelo's neighbors. He starts asking them if they've seen Angelo.

"You seen Angelo?"

"No, I haven't."

"Fuck! I mean, thanks. If you see him, could you let him know that Dimitri was looking for him."

"Sure, if I see him, I'll give him the message."

Dimitri yells out to the rest of Angelo's neighbors.

"Sorry everybody, sorry."

Dimitri gets back in his car and leaves.

Chanell's house, we hear noises of ecstasy as we approach the bedroom door. Angelo and Chanell are lying on the bed eating cannolis.

"Oh, these are magnificent."

"Pretty cool foreplay, huh?"

"With foreplay like this, I could go all night."

*"Really, now that's what
a girl likes to hear."*

They start kissing.

"Let me loosen you up a little bit."

"Funny, that's what I thought the wine was for."

Angelo grins, pulls Chanell onto her bed, they kiss.

"Lay down on your stomach."

Angelo begins to massage Chanell's back. Chanell's doorbell rings. Angelo stops.

"What are you stopping for?"

"Aren't you going to get that?"

"Avon."

*"You know this is a much better
experience without clothes."*

Chanell starts a little striptease. The doorbell rings again.

"Stray dog."

Chanell continues with her striptease. The doorbell rings a third time. Chanell is now extremely pissed.

"Somebody better be dead."

Chanell jumps up, puts some clothes on. The doorbell rings yet again.

"Hold on I'm coming."

Chanell looks at Angelo.

*"Don't move, looks at his crouch.
An inch, not a single inch."*

The doorbell ring is now replaced by pounding of the door.

*"That doesn't exactly sound like a stray
dog to me, maybe I should go to the
door with you."*

"Yeah, I guess you'd better."

"You got a ball bat?"

*"Yeah, as a matter of fact, I've actually
got a collection of them in the closet."*

"See, I knew you had some sort of collection."

They reach the closet. Angelo checks out a few before
selecting one. The pounding on the door continues. Angelo and
Chanell reach the door, he motions for her to ask who it is.

"Who is it?"

"Chanell, it's me Dimitri, let me in."

Chanell opens the door; Dimitri enters her house. He doesn't
see Angelo.

"Have you seen Angelo?"

Chanell has a dual look on her face, one as is to say, "No shit, he's right behind you" and the other is to say, "This better be good you're interrupting naughty time.

"Ah, yeah, I have.

"Where is he?"

Chanell points behind Dimitri.

Right behind you.

Dimitri turns around, Angelo tips forehead with the baseball bat, Dimitri goes into the Fred Sanford fake heart attack mode.

"Oh man, you scared the shit out
of me. Where's tonight's deposit?"

"The diner."

Dimitri gets a puzzled look on his face.

"What's it still doing there?"

"Sitting, I suppose."

"Funny, I thought you were supposed
to have it counted and at the house."

"Look, Z closed up tonight. He had a
romantic dinner planned with this
hot brunette."

"Really?"

"Yeah."

"How cute."

*"Would you both shut the
fuck up. I need that money."*

"Gambling again."

*"Ang, I don't need one of your lectures,
I need that money and I need it now."*

Chanell puts on a fake smile.

"So go to the diner, get it and good night."

Starts pushing his out the door.

"How much you drop?"

*"Let's just say nobody's going
to getting paid this week."*

Chanell becomes irate and gets in Dimitri's face.

*"What the hell are you doing gambling
other people's money for?"*

Angelo intercedes.

"Calm down. How much?"

"Ten."

Angelo shakes his head.

"To who?"

"A guy named little Johnny Lombardi."

"Dumb ass, that guy don't fuck around."

"Yeah, I saw this guy gambling missing fingers."

"Yeah, you lose a digit for every hour your late. How long you got to get the money?"

"Hours. I wasn't figuring on losing."

"People never do. Look, I'll spot you the money, but on two conditions. First, you pay me back and two, you come back, and you stick around and be more of an uncle to Z."

"Hey, I'm grateful for the loan, but I'm not exactly the mentoring type."

"That's too bad, cause Z's a hell of a nice kid and for him to have to go through two funerals in such a short time, that's a shame."

"All right, i get the point, I'll stick around."

Angelo turns to Chanell and starts to apologize.

"I'm sorry about tonight."

"Why are you sorry? If old Jimmy, the Greek over there had a little self-restraint, we'd be into some serious sweat right now."

Dimitri motions he's going out to the car. Angelo talking with Chanell.

*"I'll help Dimitri take care of this
Little thing and then I'll be back."*

"I'll meet you out in the car."

Angelo and Chanell pull each other close and kiss. Angelo heads for the door. Chanell grabs his ass as he leaves.

"Mind if I take the "Charlie Hustle" with me?"

"That's kind ironic, don't you think?"

Angelo smiles, raises the bat and leaves.

Angelo and Dimitri are driving to the diner to retrieve the night's deposit.

*"Hey, I'm sorry about wrecking your evening.
Angelo is enthralled with the bat. Pete Rose was
his baseball idol."*

"What?"

"I said, I'm sorry about tonight."

"You know, he really got a raw deal."

"Who?"

"Pete Rose."

"What are you talking about?"

"The man has the most hits in baseball of all-time and he's not in the hall of fame, that's bullshit?"

"Yeah, well he fucked up. He bet on baseball."

"Says who? And who cares, Pete Rose busted his ass, every single day he took the field. Screw major league baseball. Who the hell the are they anyway? A bunch of hypocritical millionaires and billionaires. You think those assholes don't gamble."

"I don't know."

"Hell, yes they do."

"Okay, so maybe some of them do, certainly, they don't bet on baseball."

"You're not getting the point. You don't think those guys used inside information to line their pockets.

"I suppose so, but..."

"So, what's the difference?"

Dimitri pondering Angelo's statement.

"Yeah, but don't you think the gambling thing tarnishes the image of the game?"

"No, what tarnishes the game of baseball are ballplayers who won't sign balls for kids without being paid. Greedy owners and players striking over millions and billions of dollars and stupid shit that the blue-collar guy don't care about."

They're rolling up on the diner when Angelo notices an unfamiliar car parked across the street. He tells Dimitri to stop the car.

"Whoa, pull over right here."

"Why, I can park right in front of the diner."

Angelo raises his voice.

"Do it!"

"All right."

Dimitri pulls the car over and turns off the lights. Angelo gets a serious look on his face.

"See that car over there?"

Points to the parked car across the street.

"Yeah."

*"I'm guessing your friends they
couldn't wait for their money."*

"Shit, talk about no grace period!"

Angelo and Dimitri get out of the car and walk to the back of the diner. Angelo peers into the window.

"Shit! They've got z tied up."

Dimitri becomes agitated and loud.

"What? Let me see."

Angelo covers Dimitri's mouth and whispers to him.

"*Shut up or else you're going to get Z killed.*"

Angelo release his hand.

"*Now, let me have another look and size things up.*"

Angelo sees two men, one who he recognizes. He shakes his head.

"*What?*"

"*I've got good news and bad news.*"

"*What's the good news?*"

"*The two guys in there, there not here for you.*"

"*Well then, what's the bad news?*"

"*They're here for me and
won't they hesitate to kill Z.*"

"*What do they want with you?*"

"*I think they're from my reunion committee.*"

"*So what do we do?*"

"*You still got that Derringer in your glove box?*"

"*Yeah.*"

"*Go get it.*"

Dimitri goes back to get the gun. Angelo makes the sign of the cross and is now having a talking with god.

*"Forgive me father, for I have sinned. Lord,
I know I've done some really bad things in the
past and if today's my last day, I just want
you to know I'm sorry and ask for your forgiveness
and I especially ask for forgiveness for what
I'm about to do."*

Angelo makes the sign of the cross.

"Amen."

Dimitri returns and hands Angelo the gun.

"That's not a bad idea."

Dimitri makes the sign of the cross.

"So, what's the game plan?"

*"This is what's going to happen. You're
going to go to the front door looking
for your nephew."*

"What if they don't answer the door?"

*"Get loud, they'll answer. The last thing
they want to do is draw any attention."*

"Okay, then what?"

*"Then start speaking Greek, then broken English.
Make sure you get both of those assholes to the door."*

"Okay, and then what?"

*"Give me enough time to free Z
up and get him out."*

"Do you have some sort of time frame?"

"Tell you what, give me your keys."

Dimitri hands him his keys.

*"When Z's out and safe, I'll have him set off
the car alarm, that's when you'll know
everything's cool."*

"Then we call the cops."

"No cops, I'll take care of this. Understand?"

"No?"

*"Look, they've found me. That means nobody's
safe. I get Z out of there, take care of business
and I pull a Roy Rogers and ride off into the sunset."*

"Yeah, but."

*"Listen, it's the only way.
Now let's get z out of there."*

We see Dimitri head towards the front of the diner. Angelo is peering into the diner watching the two thugs and Z. Suddenly one of the thugs leaves for the front of the diner. Dimitri is pounding on the door. Finally Thug #1 answers the door.

"We're closed buddy."

Dimitri starting speaking in Greek.

*Pragmatiká, den to skéftomai tóso polý, aftó
eínai to estiatórió mou kai écheis ton anipsió
mou stin pláti.*

Translation: Really, I don't think so jag off, this is my restaurant and you've got my nephew in the back.

*"I don't understand what you're trying
to say, you speak English buddy."*

Dimitri starts with broken English.

"My English, not so good."

Thug #1 is losing his patience and is starting to get louder in hopes that Dimitri will understand him better if he's louder.

"Look, the restaurant's closed buddy. Closed."

Dimitri starts talking louder just to piss off Thug #1.

"I look for my na few."

*"Look, we're closed, you can get your na few
tomorrow, all you want, all right, but now you
got to go."*

Thug #1 closes the door in hopes of getting rid of Dimitri. Dimitri pretends to leave. Angelo is still peering through the window. He sees Thug #1 come back. Thug #1 comes to the back of the diner, where Zeus is being held, and begins talking to Thug #2.

"What was that all about?"

*"I don't know some crazy guy
looking for a late-night snack."*

Dimitri again starts pounding and yelling at the front door again.

"Na few, na few, hello, na few, na few."

"You want something done right? Do it yourself."

"The guy don't speak no English."

"Well, lucky for him, I speak the international language."

"Oh, this I gotta see."

*"Don't worry about how I handle
this, stay with the kid."*

"He ain't going no place. He's all tied up?"

Dimitri continuing to be loud. Thugs #1 and #2 proceed to leave the back of the diner for the front of the diner. Angelo looking in on the diner. Angelo unlocks the backdoor and goes to Z to untie him. Z is at first shocked, but then realizes it's Angelo and is at ease. Angelo untying Z.

"I am so glad you're here."

Angelo motions to keep quiet, meanwhile Dimitri is keeping the two men occupied. Thug #2 becomes a little more aggressive with Dimitri.

*"Hey Buddy, the restaurant is closed. We're
fumigating in here. They got rats."*

"Na few, I pick him up from work."

*"I don't know what do to tell you pal,
the kid ain't here. Just us two fumigating."*

Angelo and Z are now at Dimitri's car. Angelo is calming Z down.

"Z, you need to calm down."

"Yeah, but they were going to kill me."

"Z, sometimes life is jacked up. Sometimes bad things happen to good people. I want you to remember what we talked about being the most dangerous weapon you got, okay. Your mind."

Points to his head.

Okay!

*"Z, I want you to count to thirty and then
set off Dimitri's car alarm, okay?"*

"Why?

"That's the signal that you're okay."

Z not really understanding but nods his head.

"Okay."

"All right, you remember what I told you?"

Points to his head again.

"Okay."

Angelo breaks from his typical mode and gives Z a hug and then heads back towards the diner.

"Angelo!"

"Yeah?"

"Can I ask you a question?"

"I'm kind of busy here kid, what?"

"What is Falocapoochia?"

It's what you want it to be. You see a beautiful woman, Falocapoochia. You order an all meat pizza, hold the Falocapoochia. Somebody pisses you off, Falocapoochia.

Zeus smiles. He now understands.

"Anything else?"

*"Yeah, thank you for saving
me and be careful."*

Angelo starts to head once again to the diner. Zeus speaks.

"Angelo!"

"Yeah?"

Zeus clinches his fist.

Falocapoochia!

Dimitri still talking with the thugs waiting to get the signal from Z.

"But he knows I pick him up."

"Look, I'd love to help you, pal, but he ain't here, maybe he left with some of his friends."

Suddenly we hear Dimitri's car alarm go off.

"Son of a bitch, mother, father, sister, brother. Maybe, that's him at the car."

"Yeah, it probably is. You'd better check that out."

Dimitri leaves towards the car, the diner door closes. The two thugs are walking back to the kitchen.

"What a pain in the ass! What language was that, anyway?"

"How do I know? What do I look like a linguist?"

They arrive at the kitchen, no Z. Suddenly there's a knock on the front door. They both proceed to the door expecting to see "The Uncle", but instead they find no one there. It's Angelo messing with them, but it also gives himself time to slip into the kitchen. They head back to the kitchen.

"I'm starting to get really pissed off. Where did that kid go to anyway?"

Angelo has snuck up on the two thugs.

"Yeah, doorbell ditching without a doorbell. What a little prick."

The thugs turn around quickly. All three lock eyes.

"Look, if it ain't the blue plate special. I would have thought you'd be halfway to BFE by now. This truly saddens me."

"Why is that?"

"A) I've got to kill you and B) …"

He draws his gun; Thug #1 follows suit.

"I'll lose all those frequent flyer miles I've been collecting trying to find you."

"You're breaking my heart."

"So, how do you want it?"

"Mono e mono."

Thug #1 looks at thug #2.

"He wants to fight us."

"You want to fight us?"

"Yeah, I'll take to both of you on."

"Give me a frickin break."

"What's the matter? No sack. No confidence?"

"I'll show you no sack, I'll kick your ass, put a bullet through your head and skull. Fuck you. How's that for confidence?"

Thug #1 puts his gun down, rolls this neck, jumps up and down. Thug #2 and Angelo look at each other. #1 is hyped

*"What's the matter? Afraid to deal with
the Gun Show? (Kisses his left biceps.)."*

Angelo motions Thug #1 to just bring it. Angelo and Thug #1 face off. Thug #1 throws a punch, which Angelo ducks. Then Angelo takes Thug #1's knee out with a kick and then deliver's a knockout blow to the jaw. Thug #2 looks at Angelo as to say young dumb and full of cum.

"So you want to play King of the Mountain, huh?"

*"Yeah, I can remember a beating or
two that I'd like to get even for."*

*"Yeah, if i remember right, you
were pretty much my bitch."*

Thug #2 is taking off his suit jacket and tie and rolling up his sleeves as the conversation goes along.

"You see my mother?"

"Yeah. She's doing good."

"The old man?"

*"He just sits on the porch talking about Tony
You, you're dead in his eyes. Anything else I
can privy you to before I kill you?"*

"No, but thanks for the update."

Thug #2 nods his head in acknowledgement as a mammoth brawl ensues. First Thug #2 getting the advantage, then Angelo, then Thug #2 and finally Angelo sends Thug #2 into Thug #1. They're both bloodied and beaten, as is Angelo. Thug #1 is coming around. Angelo has now secured both of their guns.

"Now, I finish this."

"What happened to mono e mono?"

"It's time to pay the piper."

Angelo tilts his head in acknowledgement.

"Turn around."

"What's the matter, can't kill me face to face?"

"Shut up. He's doing it this way out of respect."

"Do it!"

Both thugs turn around to receive their fate. Angelo unleashes both guns, but instead of killing them, he just unloads them into the diner. Thug #1 has shit himself. Thug #1 looks at Thug #2.

"He missed us, i can't believe we're not dead."

We see Thug #2 sniffing, then gets a that smells look on his face.

"What's that smell?"

Thug #1 now moves around. We hear footsteps. Angelo is upset, thinking it's either Dimitri or Zeus. He quickly turns around. It's neither, it's Victorio Gianelle.

"I thought I told you."

Angelo doesn't finish his sentence, turns around and looks as if he's seen a ghost. Angelo now looking at the man who had his brother killed.

"Boo! What's a matter, looks
like you've seen a ghost."

Angelo is now collecting his thought after this initial shock.

"Looks like you taken some self-help
courses and finally grown some balls. It's
too bad your brother didn't live to see it."

"I'm going to kill you."

Angelo runs towards Victorio. Victorio pulls out a gun and shoots Angelo in the thigh, which brings Angelo to the floor.

"Yeah, that's what you get
for making me shit my pants."

"Shut up, chooch!"

Angelo is writhing in pain but is determined to get back to his feet and kill Victorio.

"Would you two mamelukes get off
your asses and help him up."

Angelo refuses their help.

"What are you hoping to accomplish
by getting up to your feet.

"I'm going to kill you for Tony.

Victorio looks at the thugs.

"Pull down the shades."

We see the thugs close the shades. We now have the perspective of looking in on the diner. It's a silhouette of Angelo and Victorio. We see shots being fired from two guns, Angelo's body moving as it's being shot.

We now see Angelo's seemingly lifeless body lying in a pool of his own blood. The two thugs are now flanking Victorio to the left and to the right. Victorio walks over to Angelo's body. He is wearing gloves; he kicks Angelo's body to see if there is any response. Victorio kneels down, closes Angelo's eyes. He then makes the sign of the cross, mumbles a few words, stands up and proceeds to pull out a gun and shoots and kills both of his thugs, kneels down and puts the gun by Angelo's hand. Then walks back to his two thugs and place a gun in each of their hands. These are the guns he shot Angelo with. The crime scene now looks like a robbery. We see Victorio go to a mirror, take off his gloves, put them in his suit pocket, straighten his hair and tie up, then looks at his teeth, he hears some rattling around.

"I hate when body's do
that after you kill them."

He turns around only to see Angelo with Dimitri's Derringer in his hand. Now it's Victorio who looks like he's seen a ghost.

"Falocapoochia!"

Angelo raises the Derringer and fires a single shot, which grazes Victorio's cheek. Angelo smiles and falls down dead.

Dimitri and Zeus are back at Dimitri's house. There are no words spoken, yet the silence tells the whole story. Both are hoping to see Angelo knock on Dimitri's door or a phone call, just something to let them know he okay. The phone rings. Dimitri answers the phone. He cannot hide his despair, which doesn't set well with Zeus, who waits until Dimitri hangs up the phone.

"What's going on?"

"Angelo didn't make it Z."

Zeus put his head into his hands. Dimitri goes over to console him, but Zeus raises his head, motions Dimitri. Tears that have streamed down z's face. He whips both cheeks.

"I want to go."

*"I don't think that's such a good idea. It's
sounds like there was quite a struggle and
it was pretty messy.*

"So, did Angelo kill those guys?"

*"I don't know Z, they just said
Angelo didn't make it."*

"I need to go to the diner."

"Z, he's dead."

*"Look, I'm not a baby. Angelo was there for me,
when you were god knows where, I need go and
be there for him, like he was me."*

"Okay, settle down."

"No, I won't settle down. You should have been the one to teach me all the lessons Angelo taught me."

"Take it easy."

"No, see, that's what wrong with the world. People are too selfish and think "Sorry" makes everything alright, it doesn't. My mother died; my dad is all messed up in the head, so he trusts me with you. And what do you do? You bail on me and leave me with strangers."

"Look, my intentions were good, okay?"

"If you were just going to bail, then why even have offered to take me."

"I did it to help my brother. His world was shattered, I figured it was the least I could do."

"Uncle Dimitri, you did the very least you could do, the very least. His world is shattered. What about mine? What about Adonis? We've lost our mother."

"Z, life sometimes is unfair. Sometimes bad things happen to good people."

"That's what Angelo told me just before he went back to the diner."

"Angelo was an incredible guy."

"Yeah, he used to tell me things happen for reasons."

*"Embrace your tribulations for
they will make you stronger."*

*"When life treats you like a fourth string
quarterback on a last place club."*

"Falocapoochia!"

They share a laugh. They look at each other and shake their heads.

*"Maybe that's why I brought
you here to meet Angelo?"*

"Maybe."

Dimitri ponders the moment, then breaks back to the reality of the situation.

"Once the cops give us the okay, we'll go."

"Okay."

Chapter Twelve-Falocapoochia

Dimitri's house, next morning Zeus is totally running on empty, but has made up his mind about college and calls his dad.

"Hey Pops, yeah, i am pretty tired. Last night was kind of a wild night. How's Adonis? I miss him too. Look, I've made my decision. I'm going to go to a community college down here and checkout this college thing, to see if I like it. If I do, then I'll find a university I like and do it on my own terms. I've really got a taste for what life is all about. Live life for all it's worth, cause there's no guarantees of tomorrow. Okay, I'll talk with you later. We've got to clean up the Diner. Bye."

Olympia Diner, Chanell, Dimitri, and Zeus were coming to clean the diner. Before they go into the diner, Dimitri makes a plea to Chanell to change her mind, but she's steadfast in helping cleaning
up.

"Chanell, you really don't need to be here, it's pretty brutal in there."

"Look, I'm okay, alright?"

The three enter the diner. Chanell is taken back by bloodshed. She runs out of the diner and vomits outside of the diner. Dimitri runs out to make sure she's okay.

"You alright?"

"No, that's horrifying."

"I know."

*"The smell alone is enough
to make you sick."*

"Yeah, it's pretty nasty."

*"I'm sorry. I thought I'd be fine with all
of this, but I can't go back in there."*

"I understand, take as long as you need."

*"No, I mean, I don't know if I can
ever go back in there again."*

Chanell gives Dimitri a hug, gets in her car and leaves. Dimitri walks back into the diner. Zeus has made some coffee; he hands Dimitri a cup.

"Thanks."

Dimitri and Zeus both start on the task of cleaning up the bloodshed. We see the two working hard to clean the diner up. They then take a break.

"This diner totally reminds me of Angelo."

"Really?"

*"Yeah, I remember the first time I met
him. It was like meeting Sergeant Hulka."*

*"Yeah, I know that you mean he wasn't
exactly Mr. Personality, when you first
met him, huh?"*

*"Hey, what do you say? We change the
name of the diner to Angelo's?"*

Dimitri stops to ponder Zeus's request.

"I think that's a great idea."

Several hours later, the diner now appears ready for business.

"Looks like we're ready to rock and roll."

"Yeah. I can't think of anything else, can you?"

"Nope, oops, I've I forgot to water the plants."

*"Oh yeah, Angelo's famous last thing
to do before going home."*

Zeus gets a water jug and begins watering the plants. Dimitri takes a seat. Zeus is almost done when he comes across Angelo's camcorder, pulls it out from behind a plant.

"What's this doing here?"

*"I don't know, but it looks
like Angelo's camcorder."*

"Why would he have it behind a plant?"

*"You know Mr. Candid camera,
always videotaping something?"*

*"Yeah, I think I'll take it back to
Angelo's place and see what's on it."*

"Alright, then let's roll."

Angelo's apartment, evening.

Zeus puts the camcorder tape into a VHS transforming tape, rewinds it, and begins watching the tape. It has several different things on it. The most important, of course, is Angelo's own murder. Zeus is watching the tape, fast forwarding, rewinding, watching, fast forwarding and finally falls asleep while watching the tape, but is awakened by Angelo's voice. Zeus thinks he is dreaming, but then realizes he's not dreaming. He rewinds the tape to where Angelo is speaking about Zeus's first real romantic dinner. Now watching the tape. Zeus is shocked when he realizes that Angelo has taped the entire evenings of bloodshed.

"Oh my god, he taped his own death."

Zeus watches his whole ordeal; we see a person enter into the scene. The audio is crystal clear, but we really don't get a good visual on him. We see Victorio's image kill Angelo and then the two thugs. We never get a clear shot of Victorio. As he primps himself after the murders, he hears the noise of broken glass rattle; he looks over his shoulder and sees Angelo rises from the floor; he says a few words, then fires a single shot from Dimitri's Derringer, which grazes Victorio's cheek. Angelo falls down dead. We see a hand aim a remote at a tv set; it goes to a reporter reporting that noted mobster Victorio Gianelle was found guilty on three counts of murder in first degree. We see a shot of Victorio in handcuff being led to a squad car. We see a closeup and see a scar on his cheek, which was given to him by Angelo, with Angelo's last shot before he died. The hand changes the remote again. It's Zeus being interviewed by a reporter.

"So how does it feel to help put away
a known organized crime figure."

"Falocapoochia!"

Zeus turns the television off and yells for Heinz.

"Come on, we're going to be late for class."

Zeus picks up his backpack and he and Heinz leave their dorm room for class.

www.ingramcontent.com/pod-product-compliance
Lightning Source LLC
Chambersburg PA
CBHW071325140726
47996CB00005B/1823